Airplane Boys

Discover the Secrets of Cuzco

Airplane Boys #3

Edith Janice Craine

In this third book about the Airplane Boys, they get a marvelous new plane, which they name the "Lark" and which takes them to new adventures and serves them to good purpose in many a narrow escape.

Originally published 1930

TABLE OF CONTENTS

Chapter I
AFIRE!

Chapter II
TRACKS IN THE SNOW

Chapter III
PIGEON JUTE

Chapter IV
"THANKS FOR THE BUGGY RIDE"

Chapter V
IN THE "LAB"

Chapter VI
OUT OF THE SKY

Chapter VII
PARTS UNKNOWN

Chapter VIII
AN OFFICER'S PLEA

Chapter IX
THE STOWAWAY

Chapter X

THE FIGHT IN THE AIR

Chapter XI
AT CUZCO

Chapter XII
AMY-RAN FASTNESS

AFIRE!

"Humph! I wonder where in the name of pulverized pups that young Slick-and-Slippery took himself. He sure knew how to cover his trail up good and pronto." It wasn't the unseasonable weather that made Bob Caldwell shiver slightly as he glanced ahead at the deserted ranch which was rolling toward him. It was the recollection of that day, only a few months ago, when he had taken Sergeant Bradshaw and Allen Ruhel, the Canadian Royal Mounties, to identify the outlaws.

Staring at the empty ranch buildings, the boy experienced an uncanny feeling; it seemed to him that in the weeks which had elapsed since the Gordons, Senior and Junior, had been forced to vacate so hurriedly and abandon their schemes, that the huge property had become amazingly desolate. Drawing swiftly nearer he saw doors swinging disconsolately in the wind, and although he knew perfectly well that no such sound could reach his ears, he thought that even the strips of forest wailed dismally over their condition.

"Anyway," he remarked with relief, "the old man is safely in prison, and I reckon that Arthur had aplenty of Texas, so we don't have to worry about his turning up here again." Curiosity prompted him to take the glasses and examine the vicinity more closely. The rambly old-fashioned house in which the father and son had made their home for three years, swayed slightly. Many of its windows were broken, sections of the roof sagged, and one corner of the veranda was separated from its supporting pillar. A small shed in the back had fallen in, the bunkhouse entrance was blocked with debris, the corral fences leaned wearily, and the tall cottonwood trees that had been decorative during the summer, were stripped of their biggest branches.

"Guess they didn't do any more repairing than they had to while they lived there or it wouldn't be tumbling apart now," he suggested as an explanation. His eyes rested for a moment on the twisted bole of a gnarled oak and he thought he saw something move swiftly around its base, but he decided that it was probably a wild animal that had taken shelter there because of an instinctive confidence that its haunts would not be molested.

Caldwell had witnessed the ignominious capture of the older man and the unceremonious retreat of Arthur Junior, who had fled the country without stopping to lock the place or make provisions for the hundreds of head of stock which roamed the range. Humane ranchers had driven the cattle to shelter, and Bob knew that the sheriff or some of his assistants occasionally patroled the property on watch for signs of the return of young Gordon or any of his associates, but so far the place had been shunned by members of the gang as if it were plague stricken.

"At that, some of them might make it a hang-out as soon as they think people have forgotten or are too busy to keep an eye on it." He noted the rugged cliffs which rose like irregular saw-teeth and curved around sharply, like a protecting elbow. "From the ground the place isn't easy to reach without being observed. Well, what a nice little scare-cat I'm getting to be," he upbraided himself as he resolutely put the glasses into their case and turned his attention to the business of flying.

Bob Caldwell was the younger member of the Flying Buddies and he was returning from a hop in Her Highness to Crofton where he had done errands for his mother and picked up the mail for the three adjoining ranches above the Gordon's on Cap Rock; his own, the Cross-Bar on the Pearl River; the K-A which was the Austin's and his home; and Don Haurea's of the Box-Z. The recollection of the stirring events and the eerie atmosphere about the lonely ranch made him turn the plane's nose toward the blue dome of northwestern Texas until its magnitude and beauty enabled him to dismiss the sense of impending danger.

"We are all as safe as if we were in church," he grinned cheerfully, then, as the altitude meter read twenty thousand feet, he leveled off, and shot north. At the boy's right stretched the seemingly endless miles of level plain under an almost unbroken expanse of pure white, while at his left below the great ledge lay miles and miles of sharp hills, narrow valleys, and in the distance the Pearl River bottom. Presently he saw the timber line bounding the south of the K-A.

"Good old ranch," he chuckled. "And Jim, the blithering highbrow, is all healed up, thank goodness. He sure has deserted us for Don Haurea's laboratories." The boy gave the machine an affectionate tap but he felt no resentment over the new interests of his step-brother for he too was culling valuable information from that same source, only Bob was applying everything he learned to the immediate development of the Cross-Bar ranch. "She'll be some producer by the time I'm twenty-one." That happy date was five years off and he whistled gaily as his mind tried to visualize the achievements possible to accomplish during those years.

By this time Her Highness was soaring smoothly above the plain, and in the distance, so far north that he looked like an animated exclamation point as he skied on the surface of the frozen snow, Caldwell recognized the familiar figure of Jim Austin, his Flying Buddy and step-brother.

Austin's bright red mackinaw and flapping scarf stood out a cheery patch of color against the whiteness that surrounded him, and by the swing of his body Caldwell knew that the older boy was making an effort to beat him home. With an exuberant whoop, the young pilot waggled Her Highness' wings to let the challenger know that she accepted the dare, but she was a good sport, and although the distance she had to cover was four times as far as the skier's, she proceeded to make her handicap greater, by executing a wide circle, zooming, banking and spiraling. Bob was having a perfectly gorgeous time in the sky, and although he looked forward to joining his Flying Buddy, he hated to come down. But as he sped along, he saw that Jim stood a fine chance of making good, so after treating himself to a final climb, he leveled off again, then with the throttle wide open, he started to dive.

Jim was so close now that Bob could see him quite plainly, and he watched for his brother to pause and admire the spectacle of the rushing plane as it cut through space at topmost speed. Suddenly Jim did stop, stare up, then he waved his arms. At first Bob interpreted the motions as a signal of recognized defeat, but after an instant the pilot realized that his step-brother was trying to make himself understood and he seemed rather frantic about it. He glanced swiftly about to be sure that another plane was not in the vicinity, and discovering none, he took a swift look at Her Highness. As far as he could see the little bus was O.K. and he wondered if she had dropped her landing gear, but just then his eyes rested on the mirror which reflected the rear, and he gave a startled gasp of incredulous amazement. There was a thick trail of smoke belching along the fuselage and to the boy's horror he saw tongues of flame bursting almost to the forward cock-pit where he sat.

Mechanically he kicked the rubber, jammed the stick, fought with the controls, brought the nose up and reduced the speed. All the while his mind was busy in an effort to account for the fire, but he could find no explanation. Going more slowly the smoke no longer shot back, but began to hover forward, swirled about the cock-pit and smudged his glasses. Groping and straining at the safety strap, he shut off the motor, but it was evident that whatever caused the blaze was in the back, yet he knew there was nothing in the construction of the machine that could ignite in the rear.

According to the meter he was still seven thousand feet up, so he made a desperate effort to save the beloved plane but nothing he tried helped matters at all, and finally, with a sigh of regret, he released the strap, his fingers moved over the parachute buckles, then stopping to pick up the bag of mail and his glasses, he climbed over the rim of the cock-pit. One last glance back when the machine was two thousand feet up, the boy jumped, dropped like a plummet until he was clear, then he pulled the release and in a moment the chute blossomed above him and he began to drift easily. As the plane dropped swiftly past him it seemed to the boy as if all the joy of life was carried down to destruction in the crackling machine. He clenched his fists inside his fur mittens, gritted his teeth, then because he simply couldn't bear to witness the complete annihilation of Her Highness, he closed his eyes and paid no attention to his own landing.

"Spill some of it, Buddy!" Jim called sharply. Bob glanced about, saw that he was drifting toward the jagged tips of underbrush protruding above the snow, so spilled enough air to drop him more directly. He could hear his step-brother's racing skis as the older boy hurried to meet him. Then Jim caught him by the coat and helped the landing. "All right?" he asked anxiously peering into Caldwell's face.

"Sure." Bob was down now, and the pair of them hastened to get him freed from the chute.

"What happened to you? Who did you meet?" Jim asked quickly.

"I don't know what happened and I didn't meet anyone," Bob answered emphatically. "Is there any chance of saving her?"

"No!" Silently they stood together as the hungry flames, like a pack of ravenous wolves, consumed the helpless plane.

"Gee," Bob said finally then sank down and buried his head on his arm, while his body shook in a brave effort to keep back the sobs.

"Don't take it so hard, Buddy," Jim urged, but he wasn't feeling any too good himself.

"Gosh, I—I couldn't feel worse if it was one of the h—horses, or t—the dog. She—gosh, she was a dandy bird, Jim—nobody could ever have more fun than she gave us—it was more like having a good pal that you could always rely on, than just a machine," Bob choked.

"I know it, old man. I'd mighty like to find out what started her cooking. Have any engine trouble?" Jim asked.

"Not a bit. She ran like velvet, was going great when I was diving. It wasn't until I saw you doing a wind-mill with your arms that I thought of grief, then I had an idea it might be the landing gear I'd dropped and you wanted me to look out. I didn't find anything wrong until I saw the smoke in the reflection mirror."

"Come on over and we'll see if we can discover anything." They made their way in stunned silence, threw snow over the flames, and carefully examined all that was left of the little bus, but she was too far gone, or they were too inexperienced to locate treachery.

"When we get home, let's look over the plans. Maybe we can find a spot—some place where it might have been weak—" Bob proposed.

"I don't believe we will, but it won't do any harm. Who did you see when you were in Crofton?"

"Bill, he was going home to lunch, the storekeepers and the postmaster. Just the usual crowd," Bob answered.

"Where did you leave Her Highness while you did the errands?"

"In the freight yard where we always park. There wasn't anyone hanging around and the gate was closed. I had to climb over. Did that because I didn't want to call Bill back to open it," Bob answered, then he added, ruefully, "You'll think I'm a rotten pilot to let a thing like that happen—gosh—"

"Aw go on, you're a corking good pilot. I've got a hunch that some sneak, maybe some of those fellows that were in that jam at Don Haurea's last summer fixed it up so she'd burn slow and then get going good while you were in the air," Jim explained.

"But how could anyone do that?" Bob demanded.

"You may investigate me, Buddy. Were any kids hanging around when you took off?"

"No. No one paid any attention to me. They don't any more. It isn't like it used to be. The people see one of us drop down five or six times a week, so the novelty has worn off. Why even Bill doesn't come out any more and he used to run to meet us if we landed within sight of the place," Bob reminded his step-brother.

"That's so," Jim nodded. "What you got in the bag?"

"Mail and stuff."

"We better get home. You get on the back of the ski and we'll slide, Buddy slide! It's lucky we learned to do these things double. Someone at the house may have seen you drop and be worried to bits. Come along, Old Timer," Jim urged. He went for the bag, tightened the straps of the ski, then Bob planted himself behind his step-brother, the bag in one hand and the other on the older boy's shoulder, they got into step, and presently they were making good speed toward home. Jim was right in thinking that the blazing plane had been sighted, for they had not turned into the ranch road when they heard the jingle of bells as a team came dashing around the curve, the elder Austin standing in the bob-sled.

"What happened?" he shouted. "We saw Bob—"

"I'm all right, Dad," Bob assured him, "but Her Highness went up in smoke, gosh—"

"So long as you didn't go up with her, old man. Hop in here," Mr. Austin urged. "Want to come with us, Jim?"

"I might as well," Jim accepted. Presently the team dashed to the house, and on the long veranda, Mrs. Austin was waiting. She had taken only time enough to throw a heavy blanket shawl over her head, and when she saw the Flying Buddies, her eyes were filled with tears.

"Boys—"

"We're top hole, both of us, Mom," Bob called cheerily.

"I—I watched that plane—the smoke coming from the tail long before you started to dive—oh Bob—"

"Now, you knew I was wearing my trusty chute over me union suit," he teased, but he put his arms around her and held her tight.

"Your union suit, how long since you—"

"Go on. Doesn't a flying suit look like a step-in or a union suit?" Bob grinned as he led his mother into the house. The chore-boy took charge of the prancing team so Jim and his father followed.

"We have been lucky that the boys have not had an accident before, Mother, and really the danger, no matter what happens, isn't very great when they have first-class chutes ready at a moment's notice to land them safely. They both know enough to jump and keep out of difficulty," Mr. Austin remarked quietly.

"To be sure, and me trusty side-kick was on the job with the elongated feet to bring me over the snow in fine style," Bob laughed. They were in the living room now, both of them peeled down to ordinary clothes, and stood before her, a pair of fine looking tow-heads.

"What started the fire?" Mrs. Austin was not to be put off.

"As your devoted step-son so aptly puts it, you may investigate both of us, but I expect it was an exposed wire somewhere," Bob answered, casually.

"Did you look to see?" she persisted.

"We did, but Her Highness was too hot to do much examining, and my breadbasket too empty for me to want to linger so far away from the commissary department, namely, the eats—is dinner almost ready?"

"It'll be served in a few minutes. You hurry and get cleaned," she urged, for the present need made her forget the past danger, which was exactly what her son was endeavoring to achieve.

During the evening meal the subject of the wrecked plane was studiously avoided but not because the boys did not feel the loss of Her Highness very deeply. Through their minds flashed snatches of memory that made it mighty difficult to laugh and joke with Mrs. Austin, but they kept the pretense up courageously. However, later that evening Jim and his father were in the ranchman's office alone for a few minutes, then the boy's shoulders slumped as he stared through the window toward the starry sky.

"It's too bad, old chap," Dad remarked thoughtfully. "Any idea how it happened? I don't like to say much before Bob's mother."

"I don't understand it, Dad. From what Bob says, she was working first class, every part of her, right up to the minute that he discovered she was ablaze. If a single part had gone wrong she would have showed it by the indicators or in the reaction of the controls. I do not believe that the Kid would have missed anything. Lots of times he's quicker to locate pending grief than I am," the boy replied softly.

"Have you any suspicions?"

"Not one. He said, that as far as he knows while she was parked in Crofton, no one came near her, and she flew like a charm all the way."

"Sure there isn't some technical solution to the mystery?"

"If there is, I don't know it. I thought of writing to the manufacturers, and stating the facts, and see if they have any suggestions," Jim answered.

"Could someone have put something inflammable somewhere around the tail assembly, something arranged to burn slowly?" the man suggested.

"I've thought of that, Dad. But there isn't anyone in the state, outside of jail, who would be revengeful enough to do it. The men who were given the shortest sentences in that trial after the attack at Don Haurea's last summer still have over a year to serve—none of them—that I know of—have been pardoned."

"If any of them were I am sure the sheriff would have told us," Mr. Austin volunteered.

"Yes, he would. It's a cinch, Dad, that not more than one or two of that whole gang who were sent to prison know enough about airplanes and flying to set a trap that would go off like that. An amateur would have started the fire and let her go any old way. If the thing was a piece of treachery it was managed by an air man who didn't take any chance of his plot being discovered too soon. I can't figure out that anyone is guilty of such a mean trick, but I don't know how else it could have been done." With a sigh he turned back to the room and sat by his father's desk.

"You are going to miss it a great deal."

"Like fury. Dad, I want to get a job piloting, and save up for a new machine. Somehow, I can't see how we can get along without a plane."

"I will not agree to your giving up your studies, old man. The more you learn while you have the opportunity, the better off you will be later. I'm quite sure that mother will feel the same way about Bob. She has been most happy lately because of his interest in books."

The boy's face drew down, but he tried to accept the verdict manfully. After a moment, he drew a deep breath.

"All right, Dad," he agreed. His father smiled.

"Since you two came home this afternoon I have been doing some thinking on the subject. While we had Her Highness, we accepted her rather as a matter of course. One of you would go, at a moment's notice on an errand which ordinarily would take several times the time it took to go by air."

"Yes," Jim nodded his head but he wasn't following very closely. He was thinking that it would probably be months before he and his Flying Buddy went roaring into the sky again. It wasn't easy to be cheerful.

"This winter has started out as if it is going to be a very hard one," the man went on quietly.

"Yes, sir. It's been a long time since we had so much snow," Jim replied.

"Years. In fact, I don't recall one like it since I was a boy, but seasons are always doing the unexpected."

"Sure," Jim replied as his father paused.

"To a stock man that means loss in straying cattle and horses. Young stock get lost, sometimes it takes cowboys weeks to locate them, and often only a few can be saved. That's according to the old method. I'm going to miss getting the mail every day too. It's quite a novelty reading the newspapers when they are not weeks old, especially in winter," he rambled on.

"I'm sorry," Jim said earnestly.

"We all are. It seems to me, Jim, that Bob's idea of doing things in as advanced a method as possible is the greatest money saver we can invest in, so I think that for the present I shall purchase a new plane. It will not be quite such a splendid model as Her Highness, but it will help us out for the time being—"

"Dad!" Jim stared at his father, then he added weakly, "Even one of the cheaper ones cost quite a lot."

"Don't you think it will be a good investment?"

"Ha, ha," Jim laughed. "Why Dad, I think it will be corking. We'll save a lot of the stock and I'll fly for your paper as soon as it's off the press," he promised eagerly.

"Then we—."

"May we come in?" That was Mrs. Austin and she was followed by Bob, who dutifully held the door for her.

"You are always welcome."

"I say, Jim, Mom says that Dad got Her Highness, so she wants to get us a new crate—"

"My dear, the boy told me he was going to get a job piloting for the winter—that would never do, and I should like to—you know, it's been rather delightful—"

"Reading your newspaper before it gets old," Jim interrupted with a wide grin. "That's the same tune Dad sang to me, and he's going to get a plane for the ranches—"

"Now—my dear—"

"It's all settled, my dear," Mr. Austin assured her. "We were just discussing the details, and we like our plan so well we do hope that you will not do anything to spoil it." The two boys looked at the grown-ups, and chuckled.

"Tell you what, Jim, when the bus arrives let's teach them to be a pair of flyers."

"I believe it would be very interesting," Mrs. Austin said quickly, but her husband looked grave.

"You'll both be safe as in church," Jim laughed heartily, then he and Bob executed an Indian dance about the parents until those worthies begged them to desist.

TRACKS IN THE SNOW

The four days which followed the demise of Her Highness were sad ones and the whole family on the K-A ranch missed the convenience the little plane had afforded them. It seemed to the buddies that doing everything without the machine was far slower than they had ever realized, but they were both too busy to waste time in regret over the loss of their capable assistant. Then the morning of the fourth day brought the steady roar of an airplane as it beat its way swiftly down Cap Rock, lighting and sliding on a pair of runners until its pilot succeeded in bringing it to a halt.

"This the K-A?" he called to the choreboy who was racing to meet him.

"Yes, sir. Can you take the buggy around this way? Some horses are being hazed up the trail, they'll be here any minute, and they may get scared of the machine," he explained and his youthful eyes were eagerly taking in the lines of the new arrival.

"All right, old man, where had I better park?"

"Close to those trees, off the road." The pilot lost no time in following directions and it was well that he did for he had barely left the vicinity when a bunch of young broncs came crashing through the woods, sending the snow flying in a thick screen all around them.

"Ki-yi. Ki-yi." The air was filled with the musical cry, and the pilot, as soon as he again stopped his plane, climbed on top of it to watch the performance. He saw the broncs rear, kick, plunge and circle as they were being driven steadily forward, and the man could hear the creak of saddles, the jingle of bridles and crack of quirts as the cowboys dashed hither and yon to keep their charges from rushing off toward the enormous cliff which rose in a hundred-foot wall a quarter of a mile ahead. One young bay succeeded in breaking away. The pilot saw it thundering toward him; its eyes flaming, nostrils wide, and foam flecked about its mouth. The man was too startled and fascinated to realize his danger, then he heard another call.

"Ki—ki—ki." A cowboy, looking for all the world as if he belonged in a wonderful tale of old-time west came racing after the truant, his pinto apparently requiring no guiding, and his hands busy with a long rope which was singing over his head. An instant later the cow-pony cut in front of the plane, the rope flashed out, its loop opened and dropped over the bay's thrashing hoofs. As if the whole affair were one complete piece of perfect co-operation, the pinto braced its fore feet, the cowboy pulled back, and the runaway bay was secured.

"Bravo, bravo—what a circus!" The pilot yelled as lustily as a small boy in peanut row at a wild-west show, and then the cowboy glanced over his shoulder.

"Oh, hello," he shouted. His eyes lighted happily at sight of the plane, but he couldn't say anything more for the bronc was making a frantic effort to get free of the lariat and required his undivided attention. In a minute he was being hazed along with the bunch and finally all of them were milling around the huge corral, while the riders went about their various tasks. That accomplished, the pilot saw the pinto and its rider say something to another rider on another pinto, then the pair turned their horses' heads toward the plane.

"By George," the pilot exclaimed enthusiastically. "I didn't suppose a man could see anything like that these days. It's simply great!"

"Oh, that's nothing," Bob answered. "The snow made the range a hard feeding ground, so we are bringing the stock in."

"Keep them here all the rest of the winter?"

"Only a few that look as if they need extra care. We'll give the others a week around here, then turn them loose," Bob answered.

"It depends some on the weather," Jim added, and then the pilot recognized the young fellow who had turned back the unruly bay. "Glad you got here so quickly with the new plane."

"I'm glad that I didn't miss the show. My name's Kramer and I hope I get permission to hang around here a few days. If the fellow who is to pilot this machine is a crackerjack, my vacation is spoiled, but if he doesn't know much about flying I can send word to the firm that I must stay to teach him."

"Guess you're here for a run," Bob told him, "and you better get your message off as soon as you can. I'm the lad who has to fork the bird, and my side kick here. We both have a lot to learn. Last time I tried to do sky-riding I brought the machine down in flames."

"Gee, that was tough luck," Kramer said sympathetically. "I'll like staying around and you can be sure I'll do all I can to instruct you so nothing of the kind will happen again. You're a pretty good sport, really, because very often when a man has an experience like that he gets air-shy—is off flying for the rest of his life."

"We'll appreciate your help. I watched the kid come down and it was no party. The bus looked like a Fourth of July rocket shooting the wrong way," Jim announced. Then followed instructions and Kramer sized up his prospective students with real interest.

"You know, even if you did have an accident you look to me like the type who could be top-notch pilots if you don't get discouraged, and after all, you are both young. In a few years, flying will be as ordinary as automobiles then you'll be glad you took it up and stuck to it," he told them earnestly.

"This looks like quite an air bucker," Bob remarked as soberly as a judge. He urged the reluctant Tut close and his eyes traveled quickly over Her Highness' successor.

"It's a great machine. Perhaps you know that it's a Pitcairn mail wing. They are used a lot as mail carriers, but airmen have become interested in them for sport use. It's seven-cylinder, two hundred and twenty-five horse power. My boss said that Mr. Austin told him over the telephone that he wants a good serviceable plane for practical purposes. You could not get anything better than this. It's got two cock-pits, that can be covered in bad weather and as soon as you learn more about flying, if it's storming, you can shut yourselves up snug as a bug in a rug, and fly—"

"Flipping Flapjacks, you mean without looking at the ground?" Bob interrupted incredulously.

"Sure—positively," Kramer answered emphatically.

"Here comes Dad," Jim declared. "He's the air-minded member of the family. When the other crate cracked up he got right in touch with your firm and ordered another. Said the K-A couldn't get along without one. It's a wonder to me he didn't order a herd of them."

"That goes to show you how really progressive he is. Why most men of his generation—a lot of them, anyway, think flying is all nonsense—"

"This is Mr. Kramer, Dad. We just told him we hope he can stay a while and give us instructions in flying." Mr. Austin glanced questioningly at his son.

"Yes," Bob added. "Kramer never saw a real ranch, except from the sky. He sat here and almost let the broncs jump over him. He likes horses." Then Mr. Austin understood what was in the Flying Buddies' minds so he nodded approval.

"It will give us a great deal of pleasure to have him stay as long as he can, and I am sure that your mother and I shall feel much more comfortable if we are confident that you have had thorough instructions. It seems to me that you boys are a little slow in bringing

Mr. Kramer to the house. He has had a long trip, perhaps a hard one, and sitting here is cold work—"

"Oh, I was just telling them some things about the machine. My boss said that if this plane doesn't suit you, we'll send another model, sir, but from what you told him over the telephone, he thought this would be the best for your purpose," Kramer said respectfully.

"The men of your firm must know a good machine," Mr. Austin smiled.

"Absolutely—but the customer has to be satisfied. I don't mind telling you that we all feel kind of cocky over a telephone order—"

"What's the telephone for?" the older man asked.

"Oh, sure thing, it's to save time and all that, but there aren't many people who will buy a plane on short notice, why they want to see them all, read about them, listen to a man talk his head off, be taken up—"

"But my dear young man—it seems to me that when one wants a plane that is a great waste of energy to say nothing of time. Come in and meet Mrs. Austin and get rested."

"I'll take you up any time you can go," Kramer offered.

"After lunch," Jim answered.

After lunch the Sky Buddies listened with strained attention while Kramer conscientiously taught them the operation of the Pitcairn. The instructor carefully went from the propeller to the tail telling the name of every part and explaining each function in detail, while the boys listened with anxious frowns quite as if it were so much Greek to them. Finally Bob sighed heavily.

"One thing I like about a plane," he announced.

"You'll soon learn to like the whole bus," Kramer smiled, "but what appeals to you particularly?"

"The tail. Dogs and horses have them and they are real understandable parts," the boy replied soberly.

"Yes," Jim added, "but a dog or a horse doesn't have to have anyone work his tail for him. He manages his own rudder."

"I expect you know dogs and horses better than I do airplanes," Kramer laughed good naturedly. "Perhaps, while I'm here, you'll give me a few lessons in managing them."

"Sure," Jim agreed heartily. "We'll dress you up in a pair of slip-ins, and show you how to fork a bucker."

"Guess I'd rather watch someone more experienced do that. I say, if you want to go anywhere, we might take a hop. Perhaps the first time up, I'd better do the piloting, but you can learn a lot—"

"Mom wants some pink crochet cotton. Let's go to Crofton," Bob proposed, then added quickly, "You take Jim in with you first. I'd kind of like to sit in the back with nothing to do."

"That's all right with me—"

"Why the heck can't you let me take things easy?" Jim urged.

"Go on, you learn first. I have to get over being air-shy. Don't want my insides doing a tail spin till they get kind of used to it."

"It's a good idea," Kramer put in. "Sit in the back until we get to Crofton. It will restore your confidence. Perhaps on the return trip you can ride in front."

"Wall—" Jim drawled. "Sure that's pink crochet cotton?"

"Absolutely, I wrote it down." Bob fished about in his pocket and found a scrap of wrapping paper. "Here it is. One skein of blue twist."

"You were almost right, Buddy," Kramer laughed heartily. "Anything else she wants while we are there?"

"The mail," Jim answered.

"And the newspapers," Bob grinned.

"Fine. Let's go."

Presently the Pitcairn was soaring splendidly into the air, and in the front Jim eyed the controls. His fingers itched to take hold of them, but he braced himself and hooked his hands under his safety belt, while Kramer cheerfully did his piloting so the student could see every operation and analyze its purpose. Once in the air it wasn't so simple keeping up the pretense of ignorance and twice Austin nearly gave himself away, but Kramer was so absorbed in his task that the slips were unnoticed. However, he did feel that he was making great progress with this youngster, but he rather anticipated a more difficult time when he took Bob in hand.

There wasn't a single mishap during the trip, and finally, when they reached the little town, the pilot began to look about for the best place to land. With the blanket of snow on the ground visibility was hard, and Kramer circled over several sites before he finally turned to the boy.

"I'm looking for a place to come down," he announced through the tube.

"The cattle pen by the freight yard. It's been trampled," Jim suggested and pointed to the triangular runway. It was smaller than Kramer wished and built on a steep incline, but he didn't want the new owner to think the plane wouldn't do all that was expected of her, so he started the descent and at last landed perfectly. Austin hid a smile of appreciation at the accomplishment, and nodded indifferently.

"I'll get the yellow yarn—"

"Blue twist," Kramer corrected quickly.

"Sure. You come along so I won't get it wrong, and you can wire your firm from here, unless you did it at the house," Bob proposed.

"It slipped my mind," Kramer admitted.

"I'll wait here," Jim decided. He slid low in the cock-pit as soon as the pair were out of sight, and his mind was busy with the idea that someone—perhaps the lad who was responsible for the loss of Her Highness, might come nosing around. He wanted to give whoever it was plenty of opportunity to get close in case he was again in the vicinity. Austin kept perfectly quiet, his head well below the rim of the cock-pit.

He heard the jingle of bells as small sleighs slid by, the shout of neighborly greetings, an occasional automobile and the distant whine of a buzz-saw as it bit into huge logs, cutting them into cordwood. The boy was beginning to believe that his vigilance was to go unrewarded when he heard the thud of a pair of boots dropping with someone into the cattle enclosure; then came the cautious approach. They were coming to the plane, that was evident, and Jim got ready. Watching, with every muscle keyed to spring, he waited. There was a moment's hesitation, whoever it was stopped under the wing, then a second later a hand rested within a few inches of his face. He swung up with all his strength, caught the wrist firmly and yanked. At that there was a scraping, then the business end of a six-shooter was pointed into his face, and simultaneously he leaped up with a yell.

"What—" He stopped short and stared in startled amazement.

"Oh, that you, Austin?" The gun was slipped back to its holster.

"Sure, Sheriff." Jim was too astounded to say anything more.

"I calculated I'd find you here, and I'm right glad you dropped in to town today because I'm going to ask you to help me."

"I'll do anything I can," Jim assured him.

"Wall, it's this way. You know we've been keeping the Gordon place under observation. Got a deputy there most of the time. Maybe he's getting nutty, I don't know, he's alone and there's a sort of sameness to this here snow. He reported a couple of days ago that he thought someone was hanging out up there but he hasn't been able to fetch up with whoever it is and he ain't seen no tracks. I ain't had a minute to go and look myself, and I ain't got no one to send right now. He put in a call 'bout noon time. Said he's seen some tracks; they look like a bear's."

"There are no bears out this time of year," Jim reminded him.

"I told him the old fellows has crawled in and pulled their holes after 'em, but he says it's a big bear track plain as can be and it's round the ranch house."

"What can we do for you?"

"Wish you'd stop on your way home and see what the heck's eatin' the feller. It's Carl Summers—reckon you know him."

"Yes, sure I know Carl," Jim replied.

"He's needin' a job, and I'se needin' a watchman, sort of, so I swore him in. He rigged up a contraption—taps the wire and that's the way he reports every day to me," the sheriff explained.

"Couldn't he follow the tracks and see where they lead?" Jim asked.

"That's the goldurnest part of it. They only lead 'round in a circle. Ain't no entrance or exit, as it were. He can't find no place where they start or stop."

"That is odd. What do you want us to do?"

"See what Carl has to show you and hear what he has to say. If he seems kind o' sick, take him to your house en fetch the doctor, or if he's all right, you get in touch with me. If you take him home, ask your pa if he can spare a man to kind o' keep his eye on the place for a couple o' days till I can get someone else. I got a bee in my bonnet that young Gordon will land back there one o' these days, and I'm aimin' to catch him when he does."

"We'll be glad to stop and have a talk with him. I can telephone you from there if it's anything serious," Jim agreed.

"That's fine. I knew I'd find you here soon's I saw Bob swinging up the street. Watched you the other day when the kid came down and you were loafing here—" He broke off suddenly, and frowned. "Why the name o' hen's teeth did you make such a grab at me? Boy, you might o' got a whole round of lead in you and I'd had a fierce time apologizing to your folks."

"I was watching for a sneak—"

"Think you caught him?"

"Oh, no, I know I haven't—but say, what did you mean when you said that you saw me in the cock-pit the other day?" Jim asked.

"Saw you from my window up there. That is, I happened to look out and discovered the plane parked in the freight yard and you fussing away in the back seat."

"I didn't come with Bob the other day," Jim told him.

"You didn't come—why I saw you as plain—"

"My face?" Jim was excited. He hoped the sheriff could describe the fellow who was responsible for the loss of Her Highness.

"Wall no, can't say that I did. Saw the top of that helmet and as I know there are only two Flyin' Buddies in these parts, I reckoned it was you," the man answered, and Austin was most disappointed.

"It wasn't, and great guns I wish you'd come over then," he said with a sigh. He went on and explained about the burning of the plane and the sheriff scowled.

"Thunderation, that ain't lookin' too good." He took off his hat and scratched his head. "You-all got a hunch that plane's death—as it were—wasn't due to no natural causes?"

"That's the way it looks."

"All them guys that might be sore on you because of last summer at the Don's place is working off their grudge in jail—that is—let me see, Gordon got away—the young feller I mean, en the chauffeur chap. Humph. Maybe Carl ain't so loony. You can shoot?"

"Of course."

"Maybe it's mighty important that someone get up there to Carl fast as he can get. You take a set o' irons—I'll get 'em—one for you and one for Bob—"

"There's another chap with us—name's Kramer—he came with the new plane. I don't know if he can shoot or not—"

"I'll get three." The man hurried off and while he was gone, Bob and the instructor returned with an arm full of mail.

"Get that red—"

"Blue," Kramer corrected with a laugh.

"We have to do an errand for the sheriff." By the time the officer had returned, Jim had given his companions details of what was required and they both looked rather sober at the task before them.

"You boys know that Gordon—if you see him don't take no chances. I'm gettin' a gang together, and we'll follow pronto—fast as the automobile can bring us."

"We could take you along now," Kramer suggested.

"I can't leave the office for half an hour. Got something needs my attention here and it's almost as important as gettin' Gordon. Do you swear to do your duty as officers of the law and upholders of the Constitution of the United States? That ain't real regular, but you know what it means."

"I do," came from three throats. Then they climbed into the cock-pits.

28

PIGEON JUTE

"Hit her up, loop the sun," Bob called as he climbed into the rear cock-pit. Kramer let the motor run for a moment, then managed to smile at her performance.

"That's a motor what motes," he announced. Soon they took off and they looked most war-like with the sheriff's artillery added to their equipment. Through the minds of the Sky Buddies raced a varied assortment of possibilities regarding what they would find when they came down on the Gordon ranch. Jim rather wished that Bob was not along for if either young Arthur or any of his former associates were there no one would anticipate how much trouble awaited them. Although there was only a few months difference in their ages, Austin felt years older and was anxious that the younger boy be kept out of danger. He recalled the scheme the two Gordons had concocted and nearly brought to perfection at Don Haurea's ranch a few months ago. While Caldwell had not been hurt physically the horror of what he had witnessed had almost taken the fun out of him.

In the back seat Bob too was thinking of that day. Through his brain flashed the vision of his step-brother lying wounded and bleeding on the steps of the Bar-Z ranch house. It wasn't a picture a fellow could shake off easily and he was wishing that Jim was not going to be in this, whatever was ahead of them. To be sure, under the splendid care of the medical men and surgeons of the Don's people, his Buddy had healed and recovered with remarkable speed, but just the same being a target was a hazardous business and one couldn't expect to get off so easily very often. He whistled softly and determined that he would keep his eyes open and if possible shove Austin into the background. The plan looked good to the boy, and then he thought of something which seemed even better. When they came down he'd suggest that his step-brother fly on home and explain the matter to his father who could get a number of the men on the K-A together and join the deputies at the lower ranch. That was a great idea, and an even better one was to propose that Jim get in touch with Don Haurea. From this highly capable man's laboratories, something very effective could be accomplished. Bob had no thought of what the Box-Z owner would do, but since the difficulties of the summer he too had paid a visit to the subterranean department and had seen the workings of the super-television-radio. It was an awe-inspiring place and the young fellow knew that the proposal of getting in touch with its head would appeal strongly to his step-brother.

By this time the rugged peaks of lower Cap Rock were rolling swiftly toward them, and presently the buddies from their separate points of observation were examining the ranch through the glasses. Finally Jim located Carl Summers sitting on a projecting ledge from which he could keep a watchful eye on his territory. It struck the boy that the young deputy appeared very unconcerned. He had expected to discover Carl crouched in some out-of-the-way corner where he could not be taken by surprise, and surrounded with a battery of artillery. Touching Kramer on the shoulder, Jim pointed out the ledge where he had landed with Her Highness the day Lilly Boome and Ollie had inveigled him to give them a lift from Laville. Three minutes later the Pitcairn lighted perfectly on the strip of table rock, and Bob, eager to put his plan into operation, called:

"I say, Jim, I've got an idea!"

"Take off your hat and let your head cool," Jim advised. The younger boy got out of the cock-pit with all possible speed and was standing by the forward door before it could be opened. Austin grinned at him cheerfully.

"I don't need to, you nut. Listen, Old Timer, you fly on to the K-A and tell Dad what's doing, then telephone Don Haurea. I bet a thin dime against the State of Texas that he'll be able to do something worth while from his place—"

"But your brother can't fly well enough yet!" Kramer interrupted.

"Say, you sent that wire to your firm, didn't you, that you are going to stay here?" Bob demanded.

"Yes, but what's that got to do with it?"

"Nothing much, old man, but the Buddy and I know a lot more than you would suspect about airplanes. We'll give you a demonstration when we're not too busy. It's this way, we thought you looked like a deserving lad, and we were sorry for anyone who never got real close to a good horse, so, when you said that your firm would give you permission to stay a while, we wanted to help you—we're a pair of regular little helpfuls—ask our folks."

"I'll tell the world you are. Think I'm going to hang around here to teach you something you know? I'm not lying to my firm—"

"Gosh," Bob's face flushed. "That's right, I didn't think of it—you couldn't do that—" then he grinned—"but, look here, if you do like Texas and horses and dogs—and us—I'll bet you could sell a couple of planes to some of the ranchers. We'll introduce you around—"

"I'll bet the sheriff would buy one," Jim added. Then the frown disappeared from Kramer's face and he too grinned.

"Now you are talking. I'll get in touch with the firm and see what my boss thinks. Much obliged, Buddy, for the tip, and much obliged too for the desire to give me a good time." He held out his hand and Caldwell gripped it firmly in his own.

"Now that's settled," Jim put in—"the sheriff said that Summers has an instrument here and he has tapped the telephone wires. Your idea of getting in touch with Dad and the Don is great, I'll do it by phone."

"Oh—yes, sure you can do that." Bob's face fell and he sighed as he saw how quickly his perfectly good plan to get Austin away from the danger zone vanished into thin air. "Sure, you can do that and it will save time, too."

"Hello there!" Carl Summers, who was a stocky little Texan, came swinging carelessly up the winding trail, his face wreathed in smiles.

"Hello yourself. We were at Crofton and the sheriff asked us to drop in and see how things are," Jim explained.

"That's fine. For a couple of days I sure have been doing some tall figuring without getting an answer. Guess I was sort of hipped with the snow and the emptiness of this place, but I wasn't all goofy," he said.

"Did you find anything?" Jim asked. He and Kramer were out of the cock-pit ready to listen to the story, whatever it was.

"Yes, a spell ago. I've been feeling that I wasn't alone on this ranch and it got me worried, not because I was afraid, but because I couldn't come up with anyone. The first time was at night, I was asleep in a bunk I fixed myself in the old root house, that dugout, and I awoke thinking I heard prowlers. I couldn't find anything, but dozens of times since then I was sure I was being trailed; then I found those bear tracks and I know bears are enjoying a siesta this time of year, but they were tracks and they went around in a circle. It didn't make me feel too good trying to figure what made 'em."

"It must have made you anxious," Kramer remarked.

"Surely did, brother. I reported to the sheriff and he promised to get someone here as fast as he could, and he told me to keep watch. Now, you two know bear tracks, just for fun come and look at this set and see if you can tell what made them and where the animal came from or went," he proposed.

"Lead on, McDuff," Kramer invited.

"You got my name wrong, buddy, it's Summers—"

"I know, but that's just a quotation," Kramer hastened to explain.

"He wants you to show us," Bob added.

"Oh, I see, he's from Missouri. Well, come along."

"Do we need the battery?" Kramer asked. He didn't like toting a gun and seeing the two in the boys' belts made him feel uncomfortable.

"We've got them on, and we might as well keep them," Jim answered cautiously.

"Bring it with you, it will make you feel more as if you are in the woolly west," Bob put in quickly. Both he and Jim were sure that leaving them behind would be foolish, and although all thought of danger had been effectively dispelled by Summers, they were not taking needless chances, at least until the ranch guardian had absolutely convinced them.

Carl made his way back down the slippery trail while the three followed single file. The descent was about a hundred feet and at the bottom they started to walk easily on the thick crust across a couple of acres of open space, then they reached the back of a row of sheds which had been used for machinery, tools, and also a smithy and general catch-all. Summers removed a loose board so they went through, and then proceeded by a winding way past the numerous ranch buildings until they came to the further end where the deserted home had been erected. There were a few scrub trees around it, their branches poking up through the snow, and here and there were layers of soft snow that had not frozen because it had been jarred from the branches or blown from near-by roofs.

"Here you are." Summers stopped at the edge of a clear spot on the far side of the house, which was less exposed than the front, and protected from the colder winds by the elbow of the cliff. The three looked down quickly, and sure enough, they saw a set of tracks that must have been made by some large animal. It looked as if the beast had made the circuit twice, for most of the imprints were irregular, but many of them were distinct enough to show their form.

"I pass, what's the joke?" Kramer asked.

"They do look a little like a bear," Bob hesitated, and a moment later Jim turned to their guide.

"Is it someone who has his feet wound up?" he asked.

"You go to the head, that's it," Carl grinned. "Reckon if I hadn't been so blamed scary I'd a thought of it myself."

"Whose tracks are they?" Bob demanded.

"And why do they go around in a circle?" inquired Jim.

"Come along and see the rest of the exhibit," Carl invited.

They followed him to the root cellar, which, as they approached, looked like a long high mound of snow. At the further side, they saw the entrance, a short steep incline, with a heavy, old fashioned cellar door that fitted into a frame which was level with the ground. This opening was thrown back, so the three stepped down, Carl pulled another heavy door, and instantly the odor of a miscellaneous collection of vegetables which had been stored there for years, came to their nostrils. Coming, as they did, from the glaring white of the world outside, everything looked pitch black, but in a moment their eyes were adjusted to the change and they saw a long room with a sloping roof. Two lighted lanterns were suspended from the huge beams overhead. A rough attempt had been made at furnishing. There was an army cot in one corner, some bright blankets draped the walls, and the earth floor was almost concealed under a collection of dressed hides. A couple of home-made chairs and a table completed the items.

"Some palatial house. Where did you get this stuff?" Bob asked.

"Mostly from the bunkhouse," Carl answered.

"What's beyond that?" Kramer wanted to know. He nodded toward the further end where he saw a partition of wide planks.

"Just another hole. I went in to see. These root houses used to be divided off. When I was a kid I played here one day, and explored this place. My dad said that the first hole was small, but every year a new section was added to hold more, and some of them were used in hot weather to keep things cool," Summers explained.

"Great idea—"

"Who's this?" Kramer asked, as he jumped back quickly.

"Pigeon Jute. You boys know him," Carl chuckled. A tall slender Indian, wrapped in a grey blanket, had risen from the cot and stood staring at them gravely.

"Why sure we know him," Jim laughed. "Haven't seen you for a long time, Jute. How're the pigeons?"

"Heap good," the Indian grunted.

"When I first knew him he was trying to get a breed of birds that would be world beaters on long distance," Jim explained.

"How did you make out, Jute?" Bob asked good naturedly, but the Indian merely grunted and shrugged.

"Real loquacious, isn't he?" Kramer remarked softly, but he did feel as if he were getting a taste of the ancient west he had read of when he was a youngster.

"He's all right. When I was a little kid he used to do things for my mother and he made enough bows and arrows to destroy an army," Bob declared. He was genuinely glad to see his old friend.

"I suppose you made the tracks," Jim laughed. "You thought you would have some fun with Carl so you hopped out of a tree, or started them by jumping from where the ice is clean."

"Jumped!" came the brief explanation.

"So that finishes the mystery," Bob sighed with relief.

"Surely does. He showed up today and wanted something to eat. I was as glad to see him as if he were a bouquet of spring flowers," Carl assured them.

"I should have wanted to punch his jaw," Kramer laughed.

"You wouldn't if you hadn't seen a human being for two weeks, besides, I've got a sense of humor," Summers answered.

"We've brightened your day a lot, old man, but we've got to breeze along. Does the sheriff know what the answer is?" Jim asked.

"Yes. I just caught him when he was ready to start up here, so he called off the Reserves and went back to work. Much obliged to you all for dropping in and I hope you do it again."

"Maybe it's just as well if we stay on our side of the line a while longer, but you have skis, slide up and pay us a visit when things get too dull. You ought to rig up a radio; that would keep you in touch with a lot of fun," Jim suggested.

"I've been building one, want to see it?"

"We'd better not linger any longer, it's getting late," Bob urged. Now that the mystery was solved he began to feel that he and Jim couldn't get away from the place any too quickly, besides the short day was coming to a close and it would soon be dark. The Indian followed them outside, and strolled off unceremoniously.

"He's got some traps set in the cliffs," Carl explained. They watched the tall grey figure striding over the snow almost as swiftly as if he were on snowshoes, and soon he was lost from sight. He stepped so lightly that he didn't leave an imprint.

"How do you like being a ranch nurse?" Bob asked, just to make conversation as they hurried along.

"It hasn't been so inter—" He stopped short in his answer, and for an instant the four of them stood in startled silence. To their strained ears came an unmistakable rumble.

"Is it a plane?" Jim asked softly, but he knew it wasn't. The words were hardly out of his mouth before the rumble grew into a thunderous roar, the earth under their feet rocked as if it had a convulsion; there was a terrific boom, followed in quick succession by three more violent explosions which threw all four of them on their faces. Kramer struck an icy spot and slid twenty feet. The land behind them ripped open, a sheet of flame and smoke belched forth, carrying huge rocks, hunks of earth and ice which flew high, wide and handsome, then began to shower as far as the cliffs.

"Come on," Bob gasped. He caught Jim's collar and the two struggled to their feet. Carl was lying motionless some distance away, and Kramer was rolling as hard as he could roll toward the row of sheds.

"We'll get Summers," Jim snapped. Bending low, the Buddies raced to the prostrate guardian of the ranch, each grabbed him and then hauled him along with them toward safety. One lump of debris struck Bob's hand a hard crack, forcing him to let go, but Jim dragged harder and after a breathless stampede, the three at last reached the open door of the shed where Kramer was picking himself up gingerly.

"Don't go in there," Jim shouted. "It may come down." He thought it was safer to trust themselves to the rain of missiles than to a building which might also be destroyed and crush them under its weight. By that time Carl was gaining consciousness and he jerked himself to his feet.

"What's the mat—"

"Can you walk, old man? We've got to get out of here," Jim urged.

"Sure." Carl took a hasty glance over his shoulder and the sight of the yawning root house, to say nothing of the hail of frozen earth that filled the air, fairly put wings to his feet and he ran as fast as they could carry him. The others followed, but keeping their footing was a difficult matter for most of the time they were sliding, and several times Carl sprawled in a frantic effort to stay upright. Then Bob noticed that the direction they were taking would fetch them up quite a distance beyond the trail they must climb in order to reach the plane on the cliff.

"Buddy, Buddy," he panted. "We're out of the course." Jim heard, dug his heels to act as a brake, and skidded around. Glancing ahead he realized they could never scale the wall. He made a megaphone of his hands and bellowed.

"Summers!" But the deputy was going too strong to stop at once, so they panted after him until finally they managed to get him to listen. "We have to get to the trail."

"Oh, yes, sure!" He seemed too dazed to understand what they really meant, so they each caught him by the arms and struggled to get in the right direction. For a moment they completely lost sight of Kramer, then suddenly they heard him shout.

"Hey—stop—" They heard his gun snap and the crack of a bullet as it struck the rocks. Then sputtered a half dozen shots in quick succession, and the three paused uncertainly.

"He's attacked," Jim shouted. "Come along." They ran faster and presently they could see across to the trail. The air man was holding his right arm to one side, but he pointed with the other. The boys' eyes followed where he indicated, and in a moment they caught a glimpse of a fleeting figure leaping up the rocks of the cliff. Once, when the fellow came to an open spot, he stopped and leveled his gun, but by that time Summers' brain began to work. He fired three shots as fast as he could pull the trigger, and they struck dangerously close to the man on the trail. With a curse he leaped back into the shelter of a huge rock.

"Drop," Bob shouted, but they kept on running and were surprised that the fellow did not fire again. He might have used all his ammunition or his gun jammed. Then, suddenly above the commotion and confusion, they heard another sound.

"Suffering cats," Bob gasped.

"Sacred Cod—the plane—" Jim started to race in pursuit, and although he ran as he had never run before, he barely reached the trail before the plane moved. Bob, who could see it best, stopped to stare, and there in the cock-pit sat Arthur Gordon. He waved impudently as the machine lifted, and in less than a second he was soaring with a thundering roar of the engine into the sky.

"THANKS FOR THE BUGGY RIDE"

As the three boys stood staring in the gathering gloom at the plane that was taking young Arthur Gordon to safety, something dropped at Jim's feet and mechanically he picked it up. It was a note weighted with a hunk of ice. "Thanks for the buggy ride. A. G. Jr." He read it aloud, then gave a little grunt of disgust.

"Great boy, that. He's as lovable as a meat ax," Bob remarked. A prolonged silence followed as the group glanced anxiously about them. The explosion had spent itself; the air was cleared but the ground was covered as far as they could see with the debris that had been thrown up. Kramer, who had fallen, struggled to his feet, staggered forward, but by that time the sound of the stolen plane died away in the distance.

"We'd better see how badly you are hurt," Jim announced practically.

"Oh, I'll be all right."

"We'll make sure. Bob's a whiz at first aid, his mother taught him. Have you got any bandaging or stuff like that, Carl?"

"Had a kit," Summers replied ruefully as his eyes rested on his destroyed quarters, "but I calculate there isn't much of anything left."

"Who do you suppose started that thing?" Kramer asked weakly. He wavered a bit and Caldwell sprang to support him. "Was it the Indian?"

"I don't know, but I imagine it was the lad who stole the plane," Bob answered. "Come along to the bunk house. Wish one of you fellows would make a fire. There's an old stove in there. Rustle around and find a kettle or something so I can heat some water." They prepared to obey the commanding officer and presently they had Kramer on one of the bunks, but there wasn't any sort of cover to put over him. Jim ran out and gathered an arm full of wood, there was plenty of that scattered around, and it didn't take him long to get things ready. Carl found an old pail, but it leaked, so he filled it with clean snow and rummaged further.

"Who's got a match?" Jim asked. "I haven't."

"Neither have I," Bob added.

"I had some in the root house—"

"Feel around in my pockets, Buddy. I guess you'll find a few in a folder." The folder was located but there were only two left.

"Here's the whole stock." Bob handed it to his step-brother, who promptly whittled a good collection of shavings to make doubly sure he got his fire. When he struck the first one it crackled like a firecracker and was useless. The four watched as the boy cautiously scratched the last one. After several futile attempts it lighted successfully, a piece of shaving caught, flickered an instant then blazed up and lighted other bits. They sighed with relief at the performance.

"What next, Doctor?" Jim grinned.

"See if you can find some kind of pail or pot, to heat some water in. How many snivel dusters have you got? My patient is bleeding." Two clean handkerchiefs were produced, then leaving the patient and his attendant, Carl and Jim started to forage for a container. After a five-minute search they found a pot which was serviceable, then they filled it with snow and took it in to melt.

"Couldn't you get any water?" Bob demanded.

"No," Jim answered.

Kramer was partly stripped and the boy found that he had been shot in the shoulder. "Don't know how bad it is, but I can tie it up for a little while, then we have to find a way to get out. See what you can do." He went back to his task, and the two assistants watched his capable fingers making a temporary dressing for the wound.

"It's getting pretty dark. Let's take some dry wood for torches, then investigate," Jim proposed. He selected one of the longest pieces from the pile on the floor, lighted the end, and again the two sallied forth.

"Great guns, Jim, suppose we all had been in that place when that thing went off. We'd have been scattered over the landscape."

"In small chunks," Jim supplemented. "The sheriff told us that you tapped the wires and reported to him. Suppose we do that now. We can call K-A, his office and get a doctor here, or something like that. I didn't do any extra gabbing about Kramer, but I know Bob, and I have a hunch that the chap has been hurt pretty seriously and needs help quick."

"A part of the instrument is in the shed, we can get it and try, but I did the tapping in my dugout and that's blown to blazes," Carl answered. They were making their way to the shed, and Jim frowned at the information.

"There's a telephone, or several of them in the house—"

"Sure, but the root-house was between that and Crofton so if the wires are broken we are out of luck unless we can find an end." A few minutes later Carl found the instrument, and the pair went on to the scene of the disaster. They picked up several sections of dry wood to use when they needed more torches. Holding the light high the boys stopped at what had once been the entrance to Summers' quarters but now it looked more like a hole that had been shelled with a big gun. From one end to the other they couldn't see a thing that wasn't badly broken, or wedged so tightly it was immovable. The iron cot was a twisted mass of metal, some of the larger sections of planking stuck up out of the accumulation of earth which had dropped back, and near by they discovered a piece of ski too short to be of any use.

"You hold the light and I'll feel around," Jim suggested. "Where abouts was the place you tapped?"

"On the right side of the door. A long time ago someone who owned the ranch had all the wires put in cables underground. It's a great way to have them but if you don't know how they are placed it's some job to locate them," Carl explained.

"Yes, I know. The only telegraph poles go along the back of the K-A, so they won't help us. Can you get into the house?"

"Sure, I've got the keys—no I haven't. I left them here on the shelf in a jar this morning. Thought I wouldn't take a chance on losing them and they are kind of awkward to carry around," Carl answered. "Whoever set this off surely got us where they want us."

"We'd better break in somehow. You are an officer of the law, so you have a right to do that in an emergency. Come along and we'll see how things are inside. My family will be throwing fits about now, especially if the bang of that blow-up carried so far," Jim urged. They hurried toward the old ranch house and presently were standing on the long, low veranda. Their first try was to find out if there were any of the windows which had been left unfastened, but they were all nailed tightly.

"Here goes." Carl smashed one of the larger panes with a piece of the torch wood they carried, then he ripped out the cross sections, and in a few minutes they were standing in what had been the family living room. Considering the haste the owners had been forced to make when they took their departure, the place was almost bare.

"How do you account for this?" Jim asked in surprise.

"Can't really. I've never been in here, not since I came up to keep watch. The sheriff told me not to unless it was necessary. He said the house had been locked just as they found it and not to disturb anything," answered Carl. "Expect Arthur Gordon has been hanging around and got away with the stuff. Great Scott, I'm some watchman."

The same depleted state existed everywhere they investigated and as they walked from room to room their footsteps echoed hollowly. Carefully they both watched for telephone instruments and at last they found one in the long hall which went from one end of the building to the other but after examining it they learned that it was merely a house phone that was not used for outside purposes at all.

"That's that! I know there was a phone in this room," Jim declared suddenly making his way back to the living room. He remembered the day he had been in Don Haurea's laboratory and had sat before the television-radio watching and listening to the two Gordons. That time the phone had rung and the young man talked over it. Without the furnishings it was not easy to locate where the instrument had stood, so they lighted a second torch and painstakingly examined the floor.

"Isn't that a hole?" Carl pointed to the floor and sure enough they found an opening large enough to permit wires or a cable to go through, but there wasn't even an inch of one left.

"It must go into the cellar," Jim announced. He stood a moment to get the position, then they searched for the trap door through which they followed the stone steps down to the cave-like basement. It too had been systematically cleaned out. There wasn't a useful thing in the place. It took a few minutes to find the hole that went into the living room above, but there was nothing left of the telephone.

"Wonder why in heck he ripped them up!" Carl exploded. "What did he expect to do with them?"

"Search me," answered Jim. "I say, this place surely is spooky."

"Let's get out," urged Carl. "Think it's all right to leave Bob and Kramer alone?" he added.

"We're here, so we'd better have another look for some wires," Jim insisted. "We've simply got to get into connection with somebody soon." Later they found the place where the cable went through the masonry but everything had been ripped away, and there was no possible means of getting at the connections that had once been there.

"We're dished at this end. If I had been above the house I'd have discovered that these things were out of commission. Perhaps that's why Gordon blew up the root-house," volunteered the deputy.

"Think he did it?" asked Jim softly. The mystery of the place was beginning to get on his nerves. An almost overwhelming sense of helplessness was taking possession of him, but he struggled to combat it.

"Who else would? I don't believe it was Jute. I've known him since I was a kid. He gave me my first pair of pigeons—they were beauties," Carl answered.

"How did he happen to come around here?"

"I don't know that, but I think he was following his traps and discovered I was guarding the place. He thought he'd have a little fun with me, so he made the tracks, but he just walked in on me this morning. I sure was glad to see him, and he laughed when I told him how he got my nanny with his trick. If he had done any mischief around the place he would have sneaked off and no one would have been the wiser. Let's go and see if the doc and Kramer are all right."

"Yes, then we'll get to work on the dugout. We ought to be able to get connected with some wires there unless they are buried too tightly under that mound. I saw some tools in the shed, we can dig and chop." They were glad to get out of the house and later when they reached the "hospital" Bob greeted them cheerfully.

"My patient is comfortable," he announced with a grin. "Able to do anything?"

"Not yet, but we'll try something else. Got plenty of wood? We may be gone an hour or so," explained Jim.

"Lots. I discovered a box full, so we'll be comfortable." Kramer was lying on the bed, but his eyes were closed and he did not move.

"Asleep?" Summers wanted to know.

"Yes, just dozed off. If you find anything to eat, bring it along."

"Sure pop. I say, Bob, are those guns you have, loaded?" Jim asked.

"To the gills," the young fellow replied.

"Well, you keep them handy—"

"Shoot first and apologize afterwards," Carl advised.

"The door is a good solid one and it has a bar across," Bob told them so they realized that his labors had not made him forget to be cautious.

"So long. Meet you in the olive grove." The two went out again and in the shed they found a couple of hatchets, a spade, and a short-handled pick, which they took with them to the hole and immediately set to work to locate a weak spot in the mass. Necessity made them search thoroughly and at last they were rewarded by discovering a place where some of the beams had only a few inches of covering, which Jim industriously shoveled out of the way while Carl held the torch.

"Here she comes," Austin exclaimed with satisfaction. Summers stuck the light in the ground, the two hauled on the boards and presently had a good-sized opening.

"It lets us in toward where the door was," Carl announced and he let himself down. "I say, Old Timer, you light another torch; we'd better each have one so we can see our way and not stumble over each other."

"Rip snorting idea. Gosh all fishhooks, I'm hungry."

"There is some grub. You look at the far end, you'll find a sort of cache I made near the partition. I'll see if I can get at the wires." They started on the task but the debris cluttered the root-house so they were forced to proceed slowly, and several times they helped each other lift pieces of logs and rocks out of the way. Finally they were busy at their respective ends, Carl looking for exposed wires, and Jim trying to find some food that had escaped destruction. He had to do more chopping and hammering and, after several minutes he succeeded in clearing a wide section of the partition, but he didn't locate the cache, so he went to work again, stopping once to kindle a fresh torch, and with its bright light he discovered that he had come through the dug-out to the second cellar.

"Having any luck?" Carl shouted.

"Not much," he answered. "How about you?"

"I think I'll have it in a minute," replied Carl and he began to chop away, while Jim at the opposite end stepped into one of the older sections. Like the front of the place this too was wrecked, but not quite so badly as there had not been such a variety of things to scatter. However, one side was inaccessible, and although Jim saw nothing of special note on the other, he decided to examine it anyway. One thing which attracted his attention was a quantity of paper which looked as if some big books had been torn to bits, and some of their pages burned. Curious, Austin picked up some pieces, wondering from where they had come, then he found out, for right in front of him was an opening. Beyond the boy was a very small room which seemed to be lined with some sort of masonry. It was about seven feet square, and had projections which might have been used for shelves and seats. On the floor was more of the paper, like that which he had picked up outside, but in the poor light the boy could not be sure if it was blank or not.

"A queer joint," he muttered, but a closer examination revealed nothing more, and there was no explanation as to why the small room was there or for what it had been used. The torch was beginning to burn close to his hand, so he made his way out. They could explore it later.

"Hey, Jim, I got it. Whoopee!"

"Good work." Jim stuffed a few bits of the paper into his pocket and hurried to see what Summers had accomplished. He found that the deputy had unearthed a wire, had attached his instrument, and was listening for a response to his call. At last it came, then after a moment's delay, Carl began to put in his message.

"I say, Sheriff, Arthur Gordon, the young fellow, was here. He got away in the Austin's airplane—" There was a pause. "He blew up the place, but we're all right, except Kramer, he was shot—" Another pause then Carl looked at Jim. "He wants to know how much gas was in the plane, how far it could go." Austin frowned and thought hard, then he remembered that as he sat in the cock-pit with the pilot he had calculated that there wasn't enough to carry them more than about sixty miles.

"Not much unless there was a reserve tank, and I don't believe there was," he answered. "We can find out for sure from Kramer, if he is able to talk."

"Only a little." Then followed a series of quick questions and answers, and finally Carl disconnected with a sigh of relief. "They discovered at Crofton that they can't get the ranches up Cap Rock on the telephone and some line men are out looking for the trouble. Your father sent a message through from the Haurea place, sent it to the north station, and it was relayed back. They wanted to know what had happened to us."

"I suppose our folks are on their way down," Jim remarked, and he was mighty glad.

"Sure thing. The sheriff is going to broadcast about Gordon and have every plane watched. Too bad it wasn't earlier in the day, but the landing field will turn on the search lights. It isn't a dark night and if he has to come down for gas he'll run the risk of getting picked up." Carl put the instrument in the spacious pockets and they felt he had done a good job.

"I didn't find a blame thing to eat, but I guess we can survive until someone comes. Say, Summers, I opened a queer hole, come and look at it," Jim urged, so he led the way back to the paper-strewn section. They crawled through the opening and Carl stared in puzzled wonder.

"Great guns, I never saw a place like this before." He tapped about the wall, but made no further discovery.

"What do you suppose it is?"

"Tell you what it might be—a hiding place. Before the blow-up, I looked behind those boards and even went into the second division. It was just another place for storing potatoes, or something like that—canned fruit perhaps," Carl answered.

"What was this metal room used for? Bob's mother has a closet for preserves in the cellar at the K-A and she has one on the Cross-Bar, but they're just built-in places to keep things at an even heat, or cool, nothing like this," Jim explained.

"Sure, I know, my mother has one. Tell you what, this is an old ranch, was settled by some of the first cowmen when the country was pretty wild. It might be that the owner had this in case of a raid, a place big enough to keep his wife and children, something like that—he might have wanted to keep them safe from Indians—"

"It looks to me as if this is about five or six feet below the surface of the ground and quite a few people could stay here but not for long," Jim remarked.

"It would protect anyone who got in, from being butchered, or in case the ranch houses were burned," Carl suggested.

"Perhaps that was it, but I don't see why all the paper," Jim argued.

"Neither do I unless they had books, accounts and that sort of thing. Some of the descendants could have used it as a safe-deposit, but I haven't got another guess. Come on and see how Bob and Kramer are."

They didn't wait to do more than throw a few pieces of plank over the openings, and then with new torches they made their way to the bunk house, which was pitch dark. Jim caught Carl's arm and instinctively the two stepped as softly as the hard snow would permit. When they reached the door, Austin listened, but not a sound came from inside. He tapped softly, his heart hammering against his ribs, with dread lest some thing had happened to his Flying Buddy and Kramer. He wished heartily that they hadn't lingered so long.

"Knock again," Carl whispered and Jim did. There was a soft movement from inside, the bar was lifted carefully, and finally the door moved, but only wide enough to permit the barrel of a gun to be poked through.

"Hands up or I'll blow you up—"

"Buddy—Bob—"

"Oh, why the heck did you come sneaking around like a pair of coyotes? I heard a dozen things since you left. Come on in. Get anything to eat?" The two entered and the younger boy turned up the wick of a small lantern. "Gosh, I thought you fellows had been buried."

"No, but we got word to the sheriff," Carl explained. "How's Kramer?"

"Crazy in the head. He's been muttering and twisting around until I had to tie him down." Just then they heard the welcome honk of an automobile, and two minutes later, Mr. Austin and Don Haurea were at the door. "When do we eat?" the substitute doctor demanded.

"Right away, my boy. Your mother knew that you would be hungry—"

"God bless her, she knows we always are," Caldwell grinned, and the rest of the party laughed heartily.

IN THE "LAB"

"Humph, now I feel as if I am alive!" Bob had just swallowed the last bite of a delicious fried-chicken sandwich, and he blinked contentedly about the room. They were all in the bunkhouse at the Gordon's. Zargo, who had accompanied Mr. Austin and Don Haurea, had relieved young Caldwell of his patient, so the Flying Buddies and Carl Summers could give their undivided attention to the basket of food the rescuing party had brought with them. At that moment Kramer moved, opened his eyes and stared at the dark man bending over him.

"You are doing well, sir," Zargo said quietly. There was something very reassuring in the manner of the Box-Z's overseer, and although the man from the north had never set eyes on him before, the dozen questions that popped into his brain on returning to consciousness began to arrange themselves in an orderly array instead of a confused mass.

"Guess you are a doctor," he said.

"I know a little," Zargo admitted.

"I say, Kramer, was there an extra tank of gas in that bus?" Jim asked. "We have been trying to calculate where it would have to come down."

"Gas? Oh, no, I left the extra ones at your ranch before we went to Crofton. Thought I shouldn't need them," he replied.

"Then that chap couldn't get more than about fifty miles?"

"It would depend upon how he flew. He'll get about sixty or sixty-five; if he conserves it," answered Kramer.

"Great, then he would have to come down in Texas. Feel like eating something? There is a little left but believe me it has taken great self-restraint on our parts to save anything."

"He may have a little, then more before we leave," Zargo decided, so they arranged a roll of blankets to raise Kramer's head, and he was ready to eat.

"I can feed him, Old Man," Bob offered. "Don Haurea wants to go up the cliff to where the plane took off. When you come back we'll go home. It's been a nice large night and a good time was had by all."

"That is an excellent suggestion," Don Haurea smiled at the irrepressible young fellow. "We shall leave the officer with you," he added and turned to Carl Summers. "You are both armed, I do not anticipate further attacks, but it is always well to—as the Boy Scouts say—to be prepared."

"Yes, sir," Carl agreed, but he wasn't especially keen about being left behind, for although he had caught occasional glimpses of the owner of the Box-Z this was the first time he had come into close contact with the man who was something of a mystery to his neighbors, and more so to the natives of Crofton, so the deputy greatly regretted not being a member of the investigating party.

"You are a good soldier," said the tall man, who was, on close acquaintance, proving so very unformidable.

"Thank you, sir." Carl was immediately eager to take his part in upholding the law and guarding the wounded. The rest of the party got into great coats, wrapped mufflers about their necks, and pulled fur caps over their ears. The three men had strong flashlights, and presently they stepped out into the night anxious to explore the vicinity as quickly as possible. Their first journey was to the scene of the explosion, which interested Don Haurea very little, and finally they made their way to the trail where they began the steep climb to the ledge.

They had to exercise care, for the explosion had loosened huge chunks of rock and ice and as they proceeded Jim was amazed that the plane had not been damaged. At last they reached the spot, but as far as the boy could see there was nothing gained by the trip. However, Don Haurea made his way close to the steep cliff, which rose almost straight as a wall with several broken sections. Carefully the man investigated all of them and a moment after he disappeared into the last one, they heard him call sharply to his servant, who responded immediately, the Austins following close on his heels. To their utter astonishment they saw something huddled in a heap against a rock and as the lights turned fully upon it, they whistled.

"It—why Dad, it's Jute—Pigeon Jute. I'd forgotten him." Zargo was bending over the Indian, his capable fingers moving swiftly, then he said something to the Don, and an instant later picked the man up in his arms.

"He was shot," Don Haurea explained briefly. "We will get him where it is warm and see if we can help him."

"Shall I go ahead with a light?" Jim asked softly.

"It would be a good plan," the Don answered, so the boy led the way down the treacherous trail. Zargo might have been carrying an infant for all the effort it took, and finally they were again in the bunkhouse. Bob was too amazed for even the mildest of exclamations, but he jumped in and arranged a bunk.

"We found him near where the plane was," Mr. Austin explained. Then they waited silently while Zargo examined the Indian, and after what seemed hours, he looked up.

"In a moment he will return to consciousness," he announced, and he was right. Pigeon Jute opened his dark eyes, looked from one to the other, then tried to raise himself. Don Haurea spoke to him in his own language and the Indian's eyes lighted. After a minute, he spoke a few sentences, and when he was finished the Don nodded.

"He says that for some time he has been selling—or delivering long distance flying pigeons to Arthur Gordon. He was in the north at the time of the trouble at the Box-Z, so did not hear of it until a few days ago after he had delivered several carriers to a ranch outside of Crofton. When he learned of the difficulty he started to find young Gordon to collect his money. He trailed him to the ranch, but could not locate him until this morning. When you boys left the dugout Jute started up the trail. He was behind the cliffs when the place blew up and was coming back to see if you were hurt when he saw Gordon leap into the plane. He tried to prevent it, but was shot for his pains."

"Jute can speak English!" Jim remarked.

"Yes, but not so well as his own tongue, which is less effort while he is so weak," Don Haurea replied.

"Whistling Pigs," exclaimed Bob, "reckon that's why Gordon did not favor us with any more lead."

"Undoubtedly it is," Don Haurea agreed.

"What was Gordon going to do, or doing with carrier pigeons?" Jim wanted to know. "Are they kept on that ranch?"

"Merely shipped from there. The man told Jute they had sold the place and were waiting for the last birds he brought down."

"Shipped by rail?"

"Truck, and probably that truck will not appear in the neighborhood again. From the plane, Gordon no doubt dropped a warning, or several of them, and every trace will be obliterated at once."

"Tough luck," Jim muttered.

"How many of the wounded can be moved?" Mr. Austin asked practically.

"Both of them," was the decision. "I shall take Jute to the Box-Z."

"Kramer is booked for the K-A," Jim grinned.

"Boy, you'll have a vacation as is a vacation," Bob promised. "You can do a Caesar; wire your firm that you came, you saw, and you conquered—"

"Were conquered," Kramer corrected. "I've had a grand trimming—"

"Well, don't broadcast it, why shouldn't you have some glory!"

They lost no time in getting the two wounded men into the limousines and although Mr. Austin urged Carl to come to the ranch, the deputy decided to wait for instructions from the sheriff, so at last they drove off, leaving the young fellow alone, but this time there was no anxiety regarding his safety. Seated beside his father, Jim's eyes stared ahead and his mind was busy. He felt it was a beastly shame that the new plane should have been lost before they had had it twenty-four hours, and although they had made the trip for the mail and newspapers, the bag was now no-one-knew where and the family was deprived of its second investment. The boy was feeling too blue over the theft to discuss the matter so he resolutely tried to put it out of his mind. He thought of young Gordon, with his limited supply of gas, but he had absolutely no hope that the outlaw would be captured. In the first place, it had been hours from the time the machine took off from the cliff before the sheriff could send the alarm, and by that time Gordon would have made good his escape. There were dozens of ways by which he might replenish the fuel supply and go on to the Mexican border, or almost any place. To be sure, a description of the machine would be sent forth but that did not help matters much.

Finally the two cars reached the point in the road where the Austins turned into their own ranch house. As he sped by, Don Haurea waved to the occupants in the other car. Then Jim wondered how it was the Indian had been discovered. He recalled the man's interest in the cliff, his investigating each crevice, and the finding of Jute. Then another query popped into his mind.

"I say, Dad, is Jute an American Indian?"

"Yes, full-blooded. What made you ask?"

"Just wondered how Don Haurea knew his language," Jim answered.

"I have heard that as a boy, the Don was always interested in the various tribes and made a point of learning all he could about them. Here we are—and, oh what a shame—" He broke off quickly when he saw the house lighted from top to bottom and knew that Mrs. Austin had not gone to bed, although it was nearly morning. Before they drove to the door, it was thrown open.

"The doctor came from Crofton and is waiting," Mrs. Austin called, and a moment later the medical man came to help his patient into the house. Over the eastern rim of the mountains the first faint streaks of dawn were breaking before the buddies were ready for bed.

"Kind of rotten about the bus," Bob said softly.

"All of that," Jim replied. They turned in to catch up on some of their lost sleep and it was noon before either of them opened his eyes again. The pair joined the family for a "brunch," which was the name Bob gave to a combination breakfast and lunch. As they lingered over the meal, the telephone rang and Jim went to answer.

"Yes, this is the K-A." There was a slight pause, then, "yes, wait," "Oh, Galloping Snails, that's great, Sheriff! Will you hold the wire a moment please? I say, Dad they found the plane—"

"They did, that is splendid—"

"Did they get Gordon?" Bob demanded.

"No, not a trace of him. Dad, they have got the plane near an aviation field. It's smashed up some, but not bad, just a few little things—"

"Can they fix it?" Mr. Austin asked.

"Yes, easily, so she'll be all hunkie-dorie."

"Ask them to do it, and if they have a pilot, have him fetch it home as soon as it is ready. We are certainly fortunate."

"All right, Sheriff. Thanks a lot for calling us." Jim hung up the receiver, and everyone was eager to hear the details.

"I suppose Gordon came down in the night and sneaked off," Bob suggested.

"They haven't any idea of what happened to him. One of the airmen saw the plane roaring along and he rode beside her just for companionship. When he looked for the pilot, Gordon, the cock-pit was empty. The fellow thought he was seeing things. Then in a couple of minutes our engine conked, stopped, and began to go down, but she spun around in grand style, going forward, and finally she dropped in a nice smooth section of the plain. The mail-man followed, but she was absolutely empty when he investigated. There was a bag of things on the floor, everything seemed just as it should be, but there wasn't a trace of the fellow who started off in her," Jim explained.

"Isn't that rather amazing?" Mrs. Austin inquired.

"It surely is, Mom. I say, Buddie, was the parachute there?"

"Two; one on the front seat and one on the back."

"The third one was gone. Gosh, Gordon must have hopped overboard when he saw he couldn't get very far. Did his exit before anyone could start a search for him. She's one grand little bus—intelligent animal, to make her own landing all by her lonesome. That ought to make Kramer feel pretty cocky—some talking point for his advertising department."

"Better run up and tell him. He was feeling badly last night over the loss, and now that the machine will——"

"Be coming home to roost," Bob grinned. "I'll break the good news to him gently." He raced upstairs to tell the salesman, who was delighted and no end set up over the achievement of the machine. While they were discussing the matter, the Box-Z limousine drove up, and Jim went to admit the caller. He discovered that it was Zargo.

"I had to be in this direction and Don Haurea asked me to stop and see if you wish to return with me."

"Thanks a lot. I'll be ready in a jiffy. How is Jute?"

"Doing very well, thank you. And Mr. Kramer—"

"Top of the world," Jim replied.

"That is good news." The boy hurried into the house.

"Oh, Bob, going to the Don's this afternoon? Zargo is outside!"

"Guess not, Old Timer. I'll linger around and keep Kramer from getting rusty, but you ooze along." Ten minutes later, Jim was in the big car, which was a particularly powerful, smooth-running machine, and now it ate up the miles as it rushed over the road that wound along the edge of Cap Rock.

"Dad told me that when he was a boy this was the stage-coach road. The drivers used to go lickity-split—mostly split—and when the passengers got out most of them would be black and blue from the bumps," Jim remarked.

"Those days are not so far distant," Zargo replied. "Your father's generation has seen many changes."

"Yes, sir, from covered wagons to airplanes. Besides that there have been the cables, radio, submarines, automobiles and television. When you come to think of it they have had to do some mental jumping to grasp it all. The inventors and discoverers in these days are everlastingly lucky they were not born earlier, during the time when the mob pitch-forked everything that was different and called any kind of progress heresy. Great guns, I never can understand why those old ducks were so opposed to people using their own brains. What a lot of good men and women they cooked when half the world had to believe what a couple of fellows dictated. Zargo, do you believe there is a hell?"

"What is your definition of hell?" the man asked.

"That's a hot one. A bad place where bad people go when they are dead. Where they have to atone for their sins," Jim answered.

"And what would you classify as sin?"

"You sure are not going to commit yourself," the boy chuckled. "Well, I don't believe God punishes people for their ignorance, but if he does, there's an army—an everlasting big one—of people who have been powerful enough. I mean held high positions, inflicted torture and suffering on their fellow men, who tried to show the world how everybody could know more—like Galileo, and a lot of fellows. I'd call destroying men like that a sin."

"You would turn a great many—say standard saints, into sinners."

"Sure, why not? If they were incapable of rightly classifying their fellows, they just naturally over-estimated their own importance."

"I should say you have given the matter a good deal of thought."

"Well, I have some," the boy flushed. "You know, when you are flying, way up in the sky—through the heavens, no matter what they were doing, it does set a chap's thinking machine to working. Gosh, I'll be glad when we get our new plane fixed. When they fetch it home, Bob and I are going to take it to bed with us so nothing can happen to it—wow, here we are."

The car went purring along the drive under the snow laden willows whose long branches rustled and murmured as the breeze stirred them. It stopped before the door, which was promptly opened by the man servant, and a minute later, Don Haurea was welcoming his pupil, who lost no time in divesting himself of outer garments.

"Your step-brother, I take it, is engaged in entertaining Mr. Kramer."

"Yes, sir. He's still got some things he wants to read, and I guess he thought if he stayed at home, it would be a little easier on Mom, and Bob sort of likes to take care of sick things. It tickles him pink if he can doctor a chicken, especially if it gets well," Jim laughed, then added earnestly, "Bob's a great buddie."

"He certainly is," the man agreed promptly.

"I say, Don Haurea, did you know that Pigeon Jute was up there in those rocks? I've been wondering all night."

"Suppose we go to the laboratory and see. It is nearing the hour when I have a few minutes with my son—"

"That's so, I'd like to say hello to Yncicea, haven't done it for a week. Does he celebrate Christmas, I mean the way we do?"

"With the rest of the world he enjoys a holiday," the man nodded.

"I'm glad, because a year without a Christmas would be sort of—well lonesome."

The two went leisurely into the long, cheery living room, to the panel in the wall which was now a familiar object to Jim, but he recalled that first day the Don had opened the way to the little elevator, which had been installed during the days of the present owner's grandfather. Without waiting, the boy pressed the tiny knot, and as he did so, his mind leaped back to the summer day when the Gordons and Burnam had led a crazy mob to the ranch, and an airplane machine gunner viciously fired his deadly rounds into the house in an attempt to destroy its occupants. The whole scheme had failed because Jim had managed, despite wounds, to press his bleeding hands against a small button on one of the pillars on the veranda, releasing an invisible wall of electricity which caught the invaders. Today the door slid smoothly, the pair stepped inside and immediately began to descend to the beautifully built under-ground work and experimental laboratories. Presently they were in the long-tiled hall, the boy went at once to his own closet where he changed to the close-fitting white suit and soft sandals.

"This sure is a comfortable outfit," he grinned. The Don was ready too, so they hurried along to the turn, and finally they were admitted to the outer room, which was exactly as it was on the boy's first visit, only now the attendant smiled his recognition, and they passed inside. Here was a large class of scientific men; as before, some of them glanced up from what they were doing, while others were too absorbed to note the late arrivals. Austin nodded or spoke a soft greeting as he passed on into the Don's own department, and soon they seated themselves on a long bench before a sort of desk with a high frame at the back. Eagerly the young fellow looked up at the man, who nodded, and then Jim's fingers moved expertly across the dial until at last he sat back and waited.

Over the screen in front of him passed a slight movement which might have been water, but Austin knew that it was a film composition rolling past and in a moment he made out blurred objects which gradually shaped themselves into a back-ground of blue sky, with a rushing stream in the foreground. Shrubs and trees stood out in stately order, then a winding path which led over moss-grown rocks to a wide terrace above. Then something moved and Jim could not contain himself a moment longer as the boy he had first seen in Vermont, stepped out from the garden.

"Yncicea," he called.

"Jim, Old Scout," came the laughing response. "In Texas you are to have a white Christmas."

"We surely are," Jim laughed. "Bob's mother is crazy about it, says it's exactly like when she was a girl in Vermont—you know—"

"When she lived on the farm, by the waters of Lake Champlain."

"Right you are. Well, it's great to see you, and your father wants to speak to you. So long, Old Man."

"So long, Jim, Old Scout; here's to the membrane on your proboscis."

"Aw, go on, that's no way to say—skin on your nose," Jim laughed.

"My son has not proved to be a very good student of slang," the Don chuckled, then, for several minutes the two spoke in that strange language which Jim had not been able to attribute to any race. Finally the father and son were finished, then the man moved to the further end of the room. Again the two sat down before a dial board, but this time the screen was more like a moving picture.

"Will this be yesterday—last night, I mean?" the boy asked.

"Yes, and perhaps it will answer your question."

OUT OF THE SKY

Young Austin waited eagerly for the photo record of certain observations made every day in the laboratory. In a moment the film had rolled to the beginning of the picture and after a few preliminary scenes passed, Jim saw the buildings of the Gordon ranch appear, one after the other. There were the barns, corrals, bunkhouse, the ancient home and the root house a short distance away. Beyond, the cliff rose in ragged ridges to the strip of table land which the boy knew so well. He saw Carl Summers, the deputy, gun on his arm, and snowshoes on his feet, moving cautiously as he made his rounds of the place in search of a sign of the return of Arthur. The picture passed from the young chap to other sections, lingered an instant on Pigeon Jute following the deputy, and at last it revealed the outlaw emerging stealthily from a long, tumbled-down building. Through the open door could be seen a pile of furniture, and as they watched, Gordon returned to the room where he fell to work piling the stuff into a deep hole at the further end. That done, the young man covered it with burlap, earth, and finally snow so that it looked as if it had been undisturbed and that the drifts had come down through the broken sections of the roof.

"What do you know about that!" The boy exclaimed in astonishment, but Don Haurea was occupied with something at the further end of the room and made no reply. Keenly interested, Jim continued his observation, and at last he followed Gordon into the old root-house where Summers had made his headquarters. The sheriff's assistant was nowhere near the spot, and Gordon gave it an indifferent inspection. He hurried to the end, moved the partition, and quickly stepped inside. He went at once to the wall, which was later blown out, removed a section cleverly covered with dirt, and then stepped hastily into the strange vault-like room, where he pulled out numerous record books, ran his fingers through them as if in search for something, which he did not find. He examined the wall, then proceeded to tear the papers.

At this point the picture changed and Jim found himself watching a group of men who were apparently in some part of Don Haurea's laboratory. They too were interested in observing Arthur Gordon's actions, but that part of the record moved to another point in the laboratory, where two men were busy before a huge piece of machinery, with a complicated looking set of dials and wheels. One of the men who had been watching Gordon came close to them. He seemed to be giving some directions, and Jim saw a pointer set, other wheels turned, then a small tube of liquid was poured into a grooved opening, and the men waited. Again the scene changed and Austin saw the new airplane land on the cliff, and he watched with interest every move which he knew the four of them had made right up to the minute when they left the dug-out with Carl and Jute running on ahead. Their own part in what followed was cut off; the picture showed the men in the laboratory and as they stood before the mysterious machine they were observing the inside of the dug-out.

Gordon was coming stealthily out of the small armoured room. He stopped to listen at every step, then he heard an odd whirring and jumped forward as if he recognized the sound as a warning, or as if he had stepped on a powerful spring. He leaped furiously to the partition, sprang out, raced through the room, his hand pressed over his face, then came the rumble, the place shook, the further end boomed and heaved convulsively, while the young fellow ran for his life until he reached the cliff, tore madly toward the plane, stopping barely an instant to fire at Kramer. In a moment he was jumping into the cock-pit, but Jute caught his ankle. With an oath, Gordon kicked out and fired, started the engine and the plane leaped into the air. The Indian was in a heap on the snow but he crawled painfully between the crevices.

"Oh, now I know why you examined those crevices." The Don had joined him and he nodded quietly.

"I thought the Indian would have a camp in the woods somewhere and would get to it, but I decided to make sure before we left last night."

"Then the place was exploded from here?"

"Yes. Gordon was ready to leave and he had a bomb which he was setting. He intended it to go off while Summers was alone so the young fellow would be blown to pieces. Unfortunately we had to wait until you boys and Mr. Kramer were a safe distance away, then when we disturbed the bomb, it made a slight noise, which Gordon recognized, so he ran for his life and managed to save it. He rigged up the explosive earlier in the day and was going to start it while Carl was making his rounds, so we decided to let the destructive thing be his own undoing; it seemed the surest way of getting him."

"Did you tell the sheriff he was there?" Jim asked.

"No. In order to do that we should have to explain how we knew the fellow was there and it isn't wise to reveal to the layman something he cannot understand. We did hope to trap Gordon in such a way that he could be captured, but when he showed the determination to kill young Summers, we had to act quickly," the Don explained, then added, "I am very glad that your airplane has been found."

"So am I. We miss the bird no end."

"Well, now you understand exactly what took place, shall we turn our attention to aeronautics?"

"Yes, sir, and I'd like to watch those chemical experiments."

"Very good." Presently the boy was seated in his own corner of the great laboratory, a huge book on the table before him, and a collection of shiny instruments and test-tubes waiting for use. He glanced at the array affectionately, gave his head a little shake as he thought how much he wanted to accomplish, then he set grimly to work, forgetting everything else in the world. It wasn't until Don Haurea touched him on the shoulder to remind him that the hours had passed, that he glanced away from his work.

"Zargo will run you home," he offered.

"Thank you, sir."

The next two days were uneventful, although they were full of suppressed excitement because they were the last before Christmas, and on every huge ranch great preparations were going forward for the holiday. Kramer improved rapidly, and so did Jute, and at last the great date arrived. Homes were decorated with greens, extra bells were attached to harnesses, and cooks were putting the last touches on feasts which were to be spread in homes and bunkhouses. The repaired plane had arrived from the shop early Christmas Eve, and the Flying Buddies went gleefully off to Crofton for newspapers and mail, to say nothing of packages which had accumulated at the post office. They came back as laden as a pair of Santa Clauses, and the entire evening was spent in preparations for the next day. No word had come from the sheriff, so the boys knew that young Gordon had made good his escape. Not even a trace of the parachute had been discovered.

Every man working at the Cross-Bar and the K-A was at headquarters for the festival, and because of the tenderfoot guest, a special party was being arranged—a real wild-west affair with rodeo exhibitions such as only real wild west men can put on successfully. The Austin family, even if there were no little members, were up betimes, and Mom insisted that breakfast be eaten before presents were opened. Everybody was in high spirits, and the air was filled with shouted greetings which lingered in the clear atmosphere. The meal was barely finished when from somewhere came the familiar drone of a racing motor. The Flying Buddies glanced at each other, then by one impulse ran out to see who might be arriving by airplane. It took only a moment to locate the tiny speck in the blue which they watched as interestedly as if they were a pair of small boys. Cap Rock was too far west for them ever to see the air-mail-men, and pilots flew their planes over that section very rarely.

"Gosh, she's a bird," Bob exclaimed.

"Looks as if she's pure silver," Jim added, and in the bright sunshine the plane did look exactly like that, highly polished. She was rapidly getting nearer, but as yet they could not make out her pilot. However, they did not think much about that for the machine was two thousand feet up and the man was probably protecting himself from the cold. Without diminishing her speed she came straight toward them and in a moment they decided that she was going to pass over, but to their surprise she executed a wide graceful curve, dipped as if she were making a salute, banked, zoomed swiftly, curved again, dived and began to descend in narrowing spirals.

"She's decorated like a Christmas tree," Bob laughed. "Somebody's coming to our party."

"Somebody is a lucky guy if he owns that machine," Jim gasped in admiration. The motor had stopped and the beautiful plane was dropping lightly into the clear space only a few feet away from the house. With one impulse the boys leaped across the veranda, slid over the frozen snow, and stopped at the same moment the plane did. Then they stared at the stranger, and at length, stared at each other.

"There isn't anyone in her," exclaimed Jim incredulously. They were standing by the fuselage, the cock-pit had a special transparent cover, but no one was seated before the controls.

"See in the back." There were two cock-pits, the machine was a four-passenger, or three-passenger beside the pilot, and the Flying Buddies walked around her, but the back was as empty as the front. They even glanced at the rigging expecting to discover someone hanging on, but not a soul did they see.

"Tell you what, bet somebody lost her. Remember, that's the way our plane came down, or it came something like that," Bob declared.

"Sure. Well, we can soon find out about her. Gosh, isn't she a beauty, Buddy!"

"Boys, bring your guest inside," Mom called from the veranda. "You haven't your big coats on."

"Be with you in a minute," Bob answered.

"By George, she looks as if she might have been made for Lindbergh." It took them only a moment to find a pair of small latches on the outside of the cock-pit cover, but before they lifted it, Bob exclaimed.

"I say, if anyone jumped out of this he was mighty particular to close the roof after him."

"That's so, but perhaps it snaps shut." They lifted the cover, much as they would lift the hood of an automobile, and they saw that the main section folded into a long narrow space. Everything about the plane was brand new. The seats were heavy shiny brown leather with lighter shade trimmings. In front of the pilot's seat the control board looked, at first glance, like any other machine's, but on closer inspection they found it was equipped with several extra dials and indicators. On each side of the cock-pit were a pair of long slender glasses. There was a radio, for receiving and transmitting, speaking tube, hamper for the traveler's convenience. The mirror was the shape of a globe and it had a reflector to cut off any part, or act as a protection for the whole sphere. It looked to the boys as if the altitude meter registered not only the height above the sea level, but it would automatically change according to the nature of the territory over which it would fly.

"Why, Buddy!!!" Jim discovered a long white envelope hanging on one of the parachute buckles and he detached it carefully.

"Does it give the chap's name?"

"I'll—why Buddy!" That was all Austin could say and he held out the envelope, which he had turned over. "Look!" Caldwell stared, and read mechanically.

"'Merry Christmas to the Flying Buddies'—Flying?—Why Jim, that's—great guns—it can't be our—Say, what's inside that envelope?" Jim was already opening it. He took out a folded sheet of heavy paper that looked like some sort of parchment. Swiftly he scanned the lines, then he jumped ten feet into the air and gave a whoop which bounded and rebounded like a ball. Bob caught the sheet from his hand and read.

"Flying Buddies: Christmas

Gentlemen:

I hope to find a place in your hearts and that I shall be permitted to serve you through many happy excursions above the world. No man of your race has ever ridden in such a plane, but I am built so that you will miss none of the pleasure of good piloting. If you will be seated and replace the cover, it will be my pleasure to show you something extra in joy-rides.

I have no name, so I can only sign myself, at your service!"

"Come a-hopping, Buddy," Jim shouted. He jumped into the cockpit, but Bob hesitated.

"What is it?" he demanded.

"You haven't a coat on."

"The cabin is as warm as toast. Hustle, me brave lad, you are retarding progress, which is sinful." Bob took the second seat, which was adjusted exactly the right size and shape, and Jim swiftly closed the cover. The motor began to purr gently, like a dozen contented lion cubs, and the plane lifted, spiraling in close circles until it reached a thousand feet, then the nose was turned north and she shot forward at a speed of nearly two hundred miles an hour. Austin was busily examining the paraphernalia on the board before his eyes, while Bob was simply too puzzled to do anything more than sit back and wonder if he was experiencing some sort of fantastic dream. In ten minutes the machine was dropping lightly in the Haurea front yard, where the Flying Buddies saw Zargo and the Don waiting for them.

"You did not fear to accept the invitation," Don Haurea smiled as Jim shoved the cover from over the cock-pit.

"Not so that you could notice it," Jim declared. "Wow, what a bird."

"Glad you like it."

"Who wouldn't! Golly, Don Haurea, it's a wonderful present, but it's pretty steep—"

"Don't you like it?"

"Crazy about it."

"My son and I both feel that the several services you Flying Buddies have rendered us certainly warrant some token—"

"Token, great heavens, Don Haurea—oh, but she's a beauty. How did you send her over and bring her back?" Bob demanded.

"A very simple little instrument. You will notice one of the dials is a little different color from the other controls. It is now set, in time as it were, with a section of our plant here, and was controlled from the laboratory. You have demonstrated that part; we will show you the ordinary method of plane piloting in a very few minutes. One thing I shall ask is that you do not mention the fact that she is equipped to operate from a central power-control. There are five stations in the world from which she can be directed, and in an emergency, even though she ran out of gas she could be kept up. I'd suggest that you keep the dial turned to the lowest notch, that will tune-in whenever you are flying, and in case of accident it may save you some trouble."

"Jinks," Bob whistled.

"May I ask where the power control comes from? but I suppose it comes from here," Jim said.

"It did for today's demonstration. There are five stations in the world; four beside this one of mine. One is in South America, one in India, one in China, and the other in England."

"I suppose there are more planes like this one," remarked Jim.

"A few."

"Well, jinks—I don't know how to thank you."

"Just the same, we do think it's mighty good of you—"

"That's all that is necessary. Now, I must go inside. Zargo will tell you how she works, then I expect, although I regret that you cannot pay me a visit this morning, that you would better get back, for you are A.W.O.L., and Mrs. Austin will be anxious."

"She sure will, and Jim, they are waiting to open the packages," Bob reminded his step-brother.

"We'll hustle." It took Zargo only a few minutes to point out the different parts and explain their use. At last the two were again closed in the snug little cabin and Jim was in the pilot's seat. He had no difficulty getting home, but when they dropped down by their own house, the elder Austins were looking for them.

"See what Santa Claus brought us," Bob shouted. Then the gift had to be admired, and although the two grown-ups thought it was a pretty extravagant one, they could not protest against its acceptance.

"It looks to me as if I shall certainly have to learn to fly if the other plane is neglected for I expect that you boys will scorn my purchase," Mr. Austin told them.

"We do not scorn your purchase, Dad, but learning to fly isn't a half bad idea. While Mr. Kramer is here, why not have him give you lessons? He'll be glad to."

"And Mom, too," Bob added.

"That is an excellent idea," Mrs. Austin agreed heartily. "I have read of women doing remarkably well and I should like to try."

"Hurrah for you," the boys shouted.

"We still have unopened packages," she reminded them, so they trooped into the house, and presently were having a gala time as gifts were distributed by Bob, who was rather glad that he was the youngest member of the family, therefore entitled to that privilege.

After the feast early in the afternoon, they wrapped Mr. Kramer warmly in blankets so he couldn't possibly take cold, then he was seated on the fence of the corral from which vantage point he could have a first-class view of the rodeo put on by the men of the K-A and the Cross-Bar ranches. Jim brought him some peanuts, so it would seem like a real circus, and the young man from the north announced when the last horse had made his bow, that it was the best he had ever witnessed.

"Seeing a horse do stunts like that makes me admire them no end, but it also makes me feel that I am more at home in a plane. They do not buck and snort—"

"They don't," Bob interrupted. "I say, where did you learn to fly? In a kindergarten? The ones Buddy and I were taken up in did more kinds of fan-fishing, and jumping than any bronc."

"Well, of course they do put you through a course of stunts," Kramer grinned.

"And you have to do that for Dad and Mom," Jim announced.

"I shall be very glad to do so."

"I shall be very glad to do so."

PARTS UNKNOWN

During the two weeks which followed, the elder Austins, under the able tutelage of Mr. Kramer, and the additional assistance of their sons, became remarkably proficient in flying the ranch plane, also, the Sky Buddies became thoroughly acquainted with the "Lark," which was the name of their own super-machine. Then the salesman removed himself to Crofton, where his firm had a new plane waiting for him and he expected to demonstrate it for prospective purchasers. Already the sheriff was watching its performance with keen interest and it looked as if that worthy might become the possessor of one of the birds. Although the boys spent a good deal of time in the air, neither of them neglected his studies with Don Haurea, and Caldwell could hardly wait until spring came in order to put some of his information into practice. One afternoon, Mr. Austin came out of his office with a letter which had come in the morning's mail.

"Oh, Jim."

"Yes, sir." The boy hurried to learn what was wanted, and presently they were seated at the big desk.

"I may go to South America," the man announced thoughtfully.

"Golly, what a trip that will be, Dad," the boy exclaimed. "Be gone long, sir?"

"I do not know. It's a matter of business and I was rather hoping that my part of it could be transacted from here, but I have received a confidential letter in which one of my associates urges me to come personally and look after my interests," he answered thoughtfully.

"Taking Mom?"

"I do not believe I had better. I have no idea the sort of places I shall be compelled to visit and I do not want to take her where she may not be comfortable. There is always a risk. If it were earlier in the winter, I should not hesitate, but it is a long trip, will take weeks, and while I can rely upon my men to look after things here, I do not see how I can get back before very late spring," he said, as if he were thinking the matter over instead of discussing it.

"Why don't you go by airplane?" the boy asked. "Goodness, Dad, no sense in wasting weeks."

"Humph. That is a good suggestion, but I do not know that the air service will help me. Although, come to think of it, I read recently that they are running trips to the southern part of Chile—perhaps I can get some information on the—"

"I say, Dad, what's the matter with you? We have two planes right here on the ranch. Furthermore, you can fly yours—"

"After a fashion. I should not think of attempting anything so—"

"No, of course not. I was just thinking that you could help out some of the time. You aren't like a tenderfoot in the air. We'll take you in the "Lark"—and it will be a grand lark—"

"Well, I don't know about that," his father hesitated.

"Didn't we go traipsing all over the United States and Canada?"

"You did, and got into all sort of things," Mr. Austin chuckled. "This would have to be a very serious trip, few stop-overs, and return home just as soon as I conclude my business. I don't know about taking you away from your studies."

"We can take a couple of books along with the luggage. Now, Dad, don't be a kill joy. This business deal is important, isn't it?"

"Very important to all of us," the man admitted.

"All right, then, let's all of us get at it as fast as we can. Nothing can beat the "Lark", and with two pilots—why Dad, Henry Ford hasn't a thing on you," the boy urged.

"I guess I'd better talk the matter over with Mother."

Such a project could not be undertaken without very serious consideration and preparation. When the idea was presented to Mrs.

Austin, she, too, hesitated about letting the Flying Buddies pilot such a trip, but she did understand the importance of her husband's arriving at Cuzco in Peru just as quickly as possible, and that the shortest time by boat was eighteen days. Usually it took longer; depending upon the weather conditions. Added to that must be the time necessary to get to the nearest port, securing reservations at a season of the year when ships sailing to southern points were booked up full before leaving the north. By airplane it would take at least two weeks less, which was a big item. Bob added his voice to the plea that he and Jim be permitted to go.

"Goodness, Mother, didn't we go all over the country, find our way and come back without so much as a broken wire?"

"Yes, you did, but you got into so many adventures. Of course you didn't have anything serious happen to you, but you were in your own country, or Canada, which is almost the same, and you did not have to travel over long stretches of water," she persisted.

"It's just as safe over water as land, Mom. We'd stop at some port to be sure that everything was ship-shape before we started to cross, and it can be made in several hops, not all at a clip, as Lindbergh did. His mother didn't object, so you be a good sport, please."

"His mother must have had some awful hours. I'm sure that every minute of them seemed like a life time," she sighed in sympathy.

"Perhaps they did, but we'll be just as cautious as Lindy was. We'll have everything in proper order, and take good care to keep it that way," Bob assured her. "Besides, if Dad can get there ahead of time, and those fellows are planning to put something over on him, we'll get him there early and he can give them the laugh. Then, we'll be home in time to start things this spring."

"It won't be like when we went alone," Jim added. "Dad will be along and he will see that we do not go butting into any mischief."

"Well—" She looked at her husband. "What do you think about it?"

"The more I think about it the more it appeals to me, my dear, but I do not want to influence you unduly. As Jim says, I shall be along, it's a business trip, no sky-larking adventure, and I rather feel that our Flying Buddies will be thoroughly reliable. They must both realize that it is a serious undertaking—"

"Sure, Dad, we do; we aren't kids any more, we're grown up—" The two real grown-ups smiled at this, and although they did not dispute the argument, neither of them could agree that seventeen and sixteen were exactly mature.

"Well, probably—since we have planes and pilots it is wisdom to make use of them and not delay needlessly," Mrs. Austin finally announced.

"Atta girl!" Bob shouted. He picked her up in his arms and swung her off the floor just to prove how big he really was.

"Robert!" His mother protested, so he sat her down again.

"Gosh, Mom, you haven't called me that since I put the cat in the frying pan," he grinned.

"Did it jump into the fire?" Jim drawled.

"It did, and after Mom got through with me, I felt as if I had been sitting in it. Wow, she did wave a wicked palm! It makes me warm to think of it," he laughed.

"Dismiss such unpleasant memories. Come on, I'm going to the Bar-Z. Probably Don Haurea can give me some valuable information about air-currents and other jams."

"Flap along by yourself, Old Timer. I'm going to the Cross-Bar to look at my new hotbeds. I want to be sure I have them in order to leave, and I'll get one of the boys to look after them."

"Shall I take you along in the "Lark"?"

"No, thanks. Dad isn't using the freighter, so I'll take that, and carry some pots back," Bob answered. The "Freighter" was the name the Flying Buddies had named the ranch plane.

"I think it isn't very respectful to call the plane Dad and I use a freighter—are we the freight?" his mother demanded with assumed indignation.

"Nope," he answered quickly, "but she's a slow-boat compared to the "Lark", Mom, and before we leave, I'll clean her up spick and span for you."

A bit later the two boys took off from the open corral, and the difference in the two machines was immediately evident. The "Lark" rose, like the bird from which her name was borrowed, while the other plane went into the air at a more gradual ascent, and by the time Bob had reached sufficient altitude to set his course, Jim was becoming a speck in the distance. It did not take him long to reach Don Haurea's and leaving the bus with one of the men. He proceeded to the laboratory where he knew he would find the Don busy at work.

"Good afternoon, my boy, something I can do for you?"

"I expect you can, sir. Fact is, Dad has to go to Peru, place in the southern part called Cuzco—"

"Cuzco?"

"Yes sir, do you know it?"

"Rather."

"Well, we persuaded him, Buddy and I did, to let us take him in the "Lark", and I thought I'd ask you about—well, the best route, and the sort of air we are likely to hit, or get hit by."

"How do you expect to go?"

"Haven't had time to consider it much, but I thought of going to Southern California and down that way, or shooting across

Mexico," Jim told him. The Don pressed a button and one of the men appeared.

"Bring me the atlas, if you please." Presently an enormous book, its pages of fine quality paper, and the cover of light wood, which held the sheets together with clamps, was opened before them. The maps were the best the boy had ever seen and as he examined them he saw that land, water and air were all carefully charted so one could tell the depths of the sea, the proprieties of its surface, whether it was rugged or comparatively smooth, the direction of tides and under-water streams, also the force of the various winds and their usual course. Each section of the world was recorded in the most complete detail, and air currents marked clearly.

"Golly, what a set of maps," he exclaimed in wonder.

"They are exceptionally fine and were compiled after years of the most careful study. Now, let me see, going directly across Mexico would seem like the better course, but I advise you to go to Miami, over the Keys, to Havana, to Belize in British Honduras (you'll have no trouble finding people with whom you can talk), then to Panama, across and down the coast line to Lima. Cuzco is inland."

"That sounds like a good route." Jim examined the map carefully. "It gives us plenty of places to come down."

"Yes. A part of the way the N. Y. R. B. A. air lines have mail and passenger service."

"That's the New York, Rio and Buenos Aires line!"

"Yes. I'll have one of the boys make you an itinerary so that you can be over the water during the daytime unless you get in too big a hurry. May I ask why you are going?"

"Dad and some friends of his are interested in a project down there with some other business associates. One of his friends wrote confidentially that my father better be on the ground. He's making quite an investment," Jim explained.

"I see. I take it you expect to go and return as soon as possible."

"Yes, sir."

"Well, this route will really be the better one, and with two pilots you can stay in the air as long as you like. I have been in Peru, and don't forget to take light clothing. It is very hot, unless you get back into the mountains. Cuzco is two hundred miles from Lima and is more temperate than places west of the Andes."

"Thank you."

"Now, you better leave the "Lark" here until you are ready to start. Our men will put her in order for you, and I'll see that she has one or two extra conveniences. She is built to withstand acids—"

"Oh, we don't expect to get into any trouble," Jim laughed.

"Of course not, but if your father is planning to give his associates, some of them, a surprise, you want to be prepared. Men of this age are frequently particularly vicious if their financial plans are threatened. This is something you want to remember, and so, do not take any chances." The Don spoke so earnestly that Jim was sobered.

"It's kind of a wild country down there isn't it?"

"Parts of it, certainly."

"Not very thickly settled."

"It isn't always the isolated spots where the greatest evil is committed. Be on your guard all of the time. I do not mean for you to be stupidly fearful, but be precautious."

"I understand. Thank you, Don Haurea, and you bet I'll be glad to have all the trimmings that the "Lark" will carry."

"All right. You might study these maps while you are here, and later I'll send Zargo home with you, unless you will dine with me. I have not had young company for some weeks."

"I'll be glad to stay, but jinks, I'm in working clothes."

"Never mind that. Is the plane here?"

"Yes, sir."

"I'll have the boys set to work on her at once. When do you expect to leave?"

"Not for a couple of days anyway. I know that Dad can't start before that."

"Fine. Now, I'll get back to my observations."

"I thought I could take some lessons with me," Jim remarked.

"We'll have some prepared."

Jim bent over the maps, made a memorandum of the route the Don had suggested, a rough sketch on which he marked various items of importance, and when the man came to tell him it was time to go to dinner, the boy could hardly believe it. Half an hour later they were seated in the cheery living room, and the meal was being served. Through the first course they discussed this and that, then suddenly Jim remembered that Don Haurea had said he had been in Peru.

"It must be an interesting country, down there, sir. Did you like it when you were in Peru?"

"Very much indeed."

"We studied its history in school, and I read some extra books about the Conquistadores. Most of the writers soft peddled the old duffers, but I got a hunch they were a pretty hot lot. Pizzaro and his brothers—they were half brothers. Only one of them got back to Spain, and he spent twenty years in prison. The Marquis Francisco was assassinated, one brother was killed by the Indians, and the other was hanged. Rather a come-down from being chief moguls, but I wasn't a bit sorry for them, they were a—" Jim saw Don Haurea's face flush and was filled with dismay lest he had said something personal.

"South America, particularly Peru, has stood for hundreds of years as a monument to those men, whose ignorance, cruelty and avarice caused them to commit crimes which constitute one of the greatest blots in the history of the world," the Don said. His eyes rested on his plate, then he looked up with his usual pleasant smile. "No doubt you have guessed that my regard for the 'Marquis' as they called him, his brothers and also partner, Almagro, is not very high. They were all low born men, except Hernando Pizzaro, who was the legitimate son of his father, and as you say, the only one to return to Spain alive. It must have been galling to him to return to his native land and be treated as a criminal; he had sailed away as a great hero, had known the riches of kings, but he died in comparative poverty."

"He had it coming to him," Jim declared. He was no end relieved that he had not embarrassed his host, and he did wonder a bit why Don Haurea, who was usually so perfectly calm and self possessed, should feel so deeply about the fate of Peru and her neighbors. "I thought it was too bad Spain didn't take a tumble to herself sooner, she might have saved something from the wreck."

"She might have."

"Buddy and I were talking about those countries, those old ones. Spain had all South America, Central America, Mexico, part of the United States, Portugal, and goodness knows what else, and now she's one of the least significant countries in the world, almost. Alfonso, he's not half bad and of course he can't help what his predecessors did, but I should think it would make him want to bite nails when he thinks, if he dares to, what his country might have done in all these years."

"Probably the history of his heritage does not constitute his happiest reading," the Don answered.

"Some of those chaps had brains enough to see that the system was a blamed poor one, but they couldn't do much until the worst was over."

"A few of the men who went or were sent out were the finest of their time, or any time. They were keen enough to see that their country must lose instead of gain by the ruthless oppression of a race which was intellectually superior to their own. The destruction of public works as great as any in Spain, and the wrecking of a government under which men lived more happily than any country before or since; could only react like a boomerang against them. At the time the Pizarros invaded Peru, there was no poverty among the people of the Yncas; there hadn't been a beggar in the land in hundreds of years; every man, woman and child was trained as few were trained in the old world. There were no rats, comparatively little disease, the travelers on the great roads were guests at the depots—inns—the Spaniards called them, and there was no oppression. The poor were cared for; everyone, from the greatest to the least, worked, did his share and had plenty. They worshipped the Sun—it was their God—and they had ceremonies in their beautiful temples—but the conquerors called them heathen, destroyed the wonderful works of art—destroyed them so effectively that the world still wonders how the work was done. The great buildings were razed, the gold ripped off. One man's share was a huge gold sun, several feet in diameter, of the purest quality, and he lost it with a throw of the dice."

"Jinks, I never read that," Jim gasped. "Wow."

"It is quite true. The gold and silver workers had made marvelous vases, all sorts of pieces of service and statuary. When you are in Cuzco you can see the remains of a temple. How the stones were brought to that spot, put together, and worked, still is one of the world's mysteries. Depots were built in every province; a whole army on the march could be supplied at a moment's notice, and if disaster over-took one section of the land, it could be re-supplied very quickly from another. Runners traveled the road from one end to the other, men who were swift of foot, and news was passed back and forth in an incredibly short time."

"It must have been lovely. I read somewhere that the roads were much more marvelous than the ones built by the early Romans," Jim said.

"They were. They went over desert and Mountains, were wide and smooth, with beautiful shade trees and seats. The land was irrigated by a system which is still a mystery. In years, ten or fifteen millions of people were butchered without rhyme or reason, vast flocks of llamas were almost wiped off the face of the earth, the highways were hacked to pieces, and the guide posts set across the deserts were burned for firewood."

"The Ynca gave them a room full of gold as a ransom."

"And they strangled him in spite of their promise to set him free. He was not a particularly good man, but he was better than his captors. During the weeks of his captivity he learned Spanish. He could read, write and speak it, could play chess well, and cards. Several men who surrounded him realized that he had a fine mind. A few like Ferdinand De Soto, were greatly opposed to his death, but they were sent off to another part of the country, and while they were gone charges were trumped up against the Ynca. They killed him because they were afraid. Had those men gone to the land, expressed a desire to trade with the Ynca's people, sent Christian missionaries if they wanted to, they would have been kindly received, welcomed, and the Spaniards could have made themselves richer than their wildest dreams. The world in general would have been better and Spain might now be a great country instead of a backward, poverty-stricken one. When you are in Cuzco you will see Lake Titicaca, one of the highest in the world. It is about half as big as Lake Champlain and very beautiful. I am sure that you will enjoy seeing the country; the Andes are marvelous."

"They must be. But, jinks, I guess I'll feel a bit as you do, Don Haurea. It was a rotten shame those people got such a raw deal," the boy said earnestly.

"Don't let what I have told you prejudice you or spoil your trip. Remember, the whole land is free now, and it was through the leadership of some of the descendants of the Yncas that the different sections managed, one by one, to shake off the yoke. You'll have a marvelous experience, and remember that when you are flying safe and high, those sixteenth century men traveled horseback or on foot through leagues of unbroken forests."

"I will," Jim promised.

AN OFFICER'S PLEA

Two mornings after the decision to fly to Peru had been made, the Flying Buddies were at Don Haurea's early, but it was not bright, for it was bitter cold, and more snow was falling, or rather being driven every which way so the air was almost as thick as milk. The boys had beaten their way up against the north wind in the "Freighter" and were now listening while the Don explained the changes which had been installed in the "Lark". A long roll of waterproof chart was on a tall spool at the left side of the control board and at the other side were small hooks so that it could be stretched across and observed without obstructing the view of the dials and keys. The knob which tuned-in with the central control power was turned half on.

"I did that so that I can keep in touch with you and any time you need help we will be able to give it to you promptly. However, we shall not interfere unless you are in difficulties, and when you are, just sit back and let things alone unless you see a light across the radio."

"All right. You can talk to us and we can talk with you over the radio, but no one else can pick us up—what we say, I mean, unless we tune down into the broadcasting belt," Bob remarked in order to impress it upon his own mind.

"Exactly. The little shutter thing like a camera will throw a light two hundred feet ahead of you; but it will not light up the plane in case you do not wish to reveal yourselves. The cabins are warm, and there is a heating system which will dispel ice—prevent it from forming on the wings and weighing you down. You can take moving pictures by releasing this spring, then setting the pointer in the proper direction. The glasses we have attached above your goggles on your helmets will be more convenient to handle than heavy field ones. They have very rare lenses so leave the flap over them except when you are using them alone."

"It sure beats me how we are to get so much power with so little weight and extra luggage," Bob frowned. "I can't get that through my head."

"I know a little about it," Jim put in. "We gather up energy as we go along and store all we need."

"That's the idea. Here are a pair of caps—they are really gas masks. Slip them over your heads, helmets and all. They are soft now, but the warmth from your faces will give them body and if anyone should attempt to put you to sleep when you want to keep awake, you will be quite safe. Keep them in your pockets and put them on at the slightest provocation. Your parachutes are of dark material instead of light, and will open all around you, like life-belts. You can use them on sea and land. There are two extra ones in case of an emergency or if you should lose one."

"Good gracious. It's well Mom isn't here; she'd think we are planning to get into something awful."

"We don't expect to, but we may as well be on the safe side. We can scoot along three hundred miles an hour if we have to, but you think we'd better not do that because it would attract attention," said Jim.

"Yes. Of course your trip is unheralded, but if anyone noticed the hour you left one point, compared it with the time you reach the next, the "Lark" would immediately become the center of observation. You have a good supply of fuel, dining service if you decide to take your meals in the air, communication with the rear cock-pit; and the man who wants to sleep, if he isn't in the pilot's seat, can shove his chair out, tip it back and make himself quite comfortable. I'd suggest that when you get to the warmer temperatures that you fly low so the change from cold to hot will not be too sudden and extreme. That is likely to be very debilitating. I see that you are both wearing the emerald rings my son gave you."

"Oh sure, why, we'd feel undressed without them," Bob laughed.

"That's well. Keep them on, they may be of service. Now, that is all. I trust that you will have a pleasant trip and that you'll return in good time. We shall look forward to seeing the "Lark" come soaring up the Cap in a very few weeks. Good luck to you all."

"Thank you, Don Haurea. I guess we'll hop along. I was just thinking, no one knows about our starting, so we might put on speed from here to Miami and save some hours," Jim proposed.

"A good idea. So long."

"So long." The Flying Buddies hopped into the front cock-pit, adjusted the shelter and themselves. Jim sat before the controls, and Bob was beside him.

"I can see where I have a good nap," he yawned as he slid his seat forward and lowered the back to a comfortable angle. The engine was roaring, so was the north wind, but no one paid any attention to that. The "Lark" rose swiftly, then, with the gale at her tail she made record time to the K-A where Mr. Austin was already dressed in flying clothes, with suit case and hamper beside him. It did not take long for him to get into his place, while his wife looked on anxiously.

"Zargo will bring the "Freighter" home this morning, Mom," Bob told her.

"All right, dear, thank you. This is awful weather—"

"We'll be out of it into a summer land in a few hours," Jim laughed.

"Don't stay away any longer than you have to," she urged, and she smiled bravely, although she didn't feel one bit comfortable about seeing her men folk flying away from her.

"Not a minute," they promised. "We'll send you wireless messages every day, and postcards with the place where we stopped marked by a cross. Be good, Mom."

Presently they were again climbing into the storm and as soon as they had altitude enough, Jim leveled off, set the course south by southeast, and opened her wide. The "Lark" split through the air like a shot and an hour later had left behind her all sign of winter weather. The two boys were intensely interested in the performance of the plane and as the speed was recorded, they glanced at each other with exclamations of enthusiasm. Before noon the peninsula of Florida was stretched out beneath them, the waters rolling on either side; at one o'clock they glided down to a landing at a private airdrome the Don had recommended. A mechanic came to greet them, and he eyed the plane with unconcealed admiration.

"Some bird!"

"We think so. Don Haurea suggested that we stop here. We want to go and have lunch, replace the gas we have used, and start off in a couple of hours," Jim explained. At the mention of the Don's name, the man looked at them more closely.

"My boss isn't here but I know that friends of Don Haurea are to be given the works. I'll be glad to do anything I can for you," he answered.

"Thank you."

"Roll her up and I'll lock her in that small hangar for you. I'll give you a key and in case I'm not here when you return just help yourself. There is a filling tank in the house."

"That is very courteous." They exchanged introductions, a few words of general interest, and when the "Lark" was housed, Mr. Austin joined them. His face wore a frown.

"Didn't we make rather good time, Jim?" he wanted to know.

"Rather," Jim grinned, but he made no further explanation then.

"When do we eat?" Bob demanded. "To quote Yncicea, my esophagus feels as if my pharynx was severed."

"We'd better take you right to the nearest hospital," Mr. Austin laughed. "I'd say you must be suffering."

"Right you are, but it's a restaurant I need," Bob declared.

"There is a very good hotel, any number of them in fact, but one I think is pretty good about a mile from here. I'm sending one of our men up that way in the car. If you care to go along he'll give you a lift."

"That is very kind, thank you so much," Mr. Austin accepted. It did not take long to get the "Lark" stored and locked in, then the party went with the chauffeur for the drive into the lovely city. The hotel looked most attractive, and the travelers decided it was exactly what they were looking for. Presently they were seated in an out-of-door dining room, and when they had given their orders Mr. Austin again broached the subject of their speed.

"Didn't we make the trip in rather short order?" he asked.

"Yes, we did, Dad. Don Haurea fixed the "Lark" so that she has extra capacity, but we are not broadcasting the fact. Besides that, we flew high and almost straight."

"And we didn't meet a bump," Bob added. "Holy smoke, winter underwear isn't so good in Miami." He began to squirm and the others watched with sympathetic amusement.

"Suppose we buy some lighter things while we are here," Dad proposed.

"Corking idea," Bob agreed. "You can't get them too light for me."

"You fellows go shopping when we finish lunch, and I'll go back to the drome. I want to have a look at the "Lark" and fill her up," Jim told them.

"Come to think of it, didn't Mom put lighter suits in the bag?"

"Yes, but just suits. She said we might need to buy extra ones and we may as well do it while we are here," Mr. Austin told them.

By that time the waiter appeared and the three gave their undivided attention to the meal, which was a particularly tasty one. There were a great many people in the place and they looked as if they hailed from all parts of the world. The helmets of the three Texans attracted some attention to their table and a few of the people smiled in a friendly fashion as if flyers were everybody's comrades. When they were about half finished a party of two gentlemen and a young lady took the nearest places. The girl looked as if she were mighty disappointed over something and Jim heard her remarks.

"I think it's a shame my brother could not be here," she said.

"It sure is, Lillian, but the Marines down below us haven't been given any leave for several weeks. They have to keep right on the job while things look nasty," one of the men explained.

"Yes, of course, but I did hope Phil could make it. It's been months since he could get away."

"He'll get extra time later. Be a good sport and try to get along with just us. We're really not half bad companions if you'll give us a chance," the man said gravely.

"You are both perfect dears. I've been so disgruntled that it's a wonder you haven't wanted to drop me into the Gulf. I'll try and make amends." She laughed gayly and her companions joined in heartily. After that the three seemed to have a very jolly time, and Jim forgot all about them. He was thinking of Don Haurea and his warning for them to be on the alert, and that was one reason he was anxious to get back to the drome and into the air as quickly as he could.

"I'd better reserve a room," Mr. Austin suggested.

"Let's go on, Dad. We can make Havana before dark," Jim said quickly.

"That's rather a long stretch of flying, my boy. I thought we would rest here, and go on in the morning."

"Bob got a nap on the way, so he can relieve me, and the quicker we get off, the better. I don't want to hang around here if we do not have to."

"I'm sure that I don't," his father admitted.

"It's unanimous. Let's hurry and get something that feels like no shirt, and be on our way," Bob urged. There was no objection to this, so they paid their bill, Jim got a taxi to take him back to the drome, while his father and Caldwell took another to expedite their shopping tour.

In due time young Austin was unlocking the hangar, and he gave the "Lark" a careful examination, then replenished the fuel supply, tried out the engine, and finally rolled the plane down the runway. One of the mechanics offered his assistance, which the boy declined for he didn't really need help and he didn't want an outsider to play nursemaid to his bus. Everything was in apple pie order when a taxi drove up with Mr. Austin and Bob, and Jim noticed a third man, who was in the uniform of an officer of the Marines.

"We got a dozen sets of cob-webs, Old Timer," Bob called.

"I'll change into mine right away." The two were coming toward him, and Mr. Austin handed a small package to his son.

"I have the extra suits in another bundle to put with the luggage. Jim, we met Lieutenant Morrow of the Marines. He is in a very unfortunate predicament, my son, and wants us to give him a lift across to Havana so he can join his company. He has been on leave, but he missed the N. Y. R. B. A. air line, and he cannot get a boat. It is very important that he join his company tonight," Mr. Austin explained as he introduced them.

"Didn't know there were any Marines in Havana," Jim remarked as he greeted the officer.

"There aren't, but I can get a lift from there without any trouble," Lieutenant Morrow explained. "You see, I got five-day's leave because my wife was sick. She's been in a bad way and I stayed with her until the last minute. I wanted to be with her every minute that I could. Then the train I took to get here was delayed," Morrow said. His face wore an anxious expression, and his eyes looked as if he had lost a week's sleep, but Jim hesitated.

"He asked us if we were flying to Cuba and told us the trouble he's in. It is serious, you know Jim, if he doesn't join his company when he's supposed to. I told him that you have been doing the piloting and I do not know how much weight we are carrying," Bob explained. Jim could see that both his Buddy and his father were anxious to accommodate the stranded Marine and he frowned.

"Mighty sorry, old man, not to be able to help you out. I'd do it in a minute, but our plane is not very big and I've just tanked up to the last ounce we'll carry," he said with emphasis. Bob looked at him, but Jim busied himself about the machine.

"Can't you dump out the extra stuff?" Morrow urged. He had fully expected to be taken and he showed his resentment. "I'm an officer of our Federal Government and you are in duty bound to assist me. I can order you to do so—"

"How do you get that way, Old Man?" Jim demanded, whirling on him quickly. "Am I responsible because you over-stay your leave? Florida has any number of air planes and you'll have no trouble getting one to take you across if you need to go. Get in, Bob and Dad." He snapped out the last words so sharply, that his two companions complied without question, and it wasn't until they were in their seats that it occurred to them that they had treated a United States officer rather sharply, but the "Lark" was already thundering into the sky. She climbed to ten thousand feet, then leveled off, and her nose was turned south.

"Come on, old man, change seats with me," Bob insisted.

"All right," Jim agreed, then he spoke into the tube. "O.K. back there, Dad?"

"Yes I am, my son, but I do not understand why you chose to be so uncivil to that officer."

"I wasn't until he began to shave-tail me, and besides, if we dropped down on one of the islands tonight and found you nicely strangled back there, your wife would never let us take you out again. We're not taking any chances," he answered.

"Have you any reason to believe the man was misrepresenting himself?"

"A frail one. While we were at lunch I heard a pretty girl almost cry because her brother, who is a Marine, hadn't been able to get leave in weeks, and another thing, I bet a gold tooth that the boat service from Miami to Cuba is better than the train service from New York to Chicago," he answered. "I'm going to change my togs."

"You surely have a mind in the making, oh my step-brother. I was so busy feeling sorry for the poor goop that I didn't use my think machine at all," Bob remarked ruefully.

"Well, use it now, old fellow. In a few minutes Neptune will be under us and he's a jealous God. Fly high, wide and handsome," Jim chuckled.

Bob turned his entire attention to flying, while Jim managed to maneuver out of his heavy clothes and get into the lighter garments. It was pretty close quarters, but it was accomplished at last, and Austin settled himself in his seat, took a look at the parachute, adjusted that and the safety strap, then he had time to observe the vast expanse of ocean rolling in endless white-tipped billows beneath them. The plane was singing along smoothly, there were only a few clouds in the blue dome above, but the wind was strong.

Austin scrutinized the chart, did some calculating, and finally made a decision.

"I say, Buddy," he spoke into the tube and Bob took the other end.

"What say?"

"If the esteemed Lieutenant Morrow was on mischief bent he will manage somehow to get word ahead of our coming. By the way, how did you happen to run into him?"

"We were just coming out of the store and he spoke to us. Said he could tell that we were traveling by plane because we had on the helmets, and he wanted to know if we could carry an extra passenger. He told us his tale of woe and finished up by saying that he was desperate to get back to his company because the Marines are busy lads right now, besides it would go hard with him if he didn't put in an appearance on schedule," Bob explained.

"I see. Well, you know Dad hopes to forestall any crookedness that may be afoot when he lands in Cuzco. It's a big deal they are putting over, the parents are involved heavily financially, and if a few of those lads who are in a hurry to get things cleaned up found out that Dad is flying to the scene of the massacre-to-be they might try to clip our wings; do something to keep him away until it's too late," Jim announced.

"Yes, that's clear, but who the heck knew we started?"

"Search me, but if Morrow was trying to put one over on us between Miami and Cuba, he'll let his boss know that we didn't fall so well for his sob stuff. They'll work fast, do something else."

"Do you believe Morrow was not on the level really?"

"I don't know whether to believe it or not, but it's just as well not to give him a chance."

"The more I think of him, the fishier he gets. Got a plan to upset his apple cart in Havana?" Bob inquired.

"Yes."

"Shoot. What is it?"

"We won't land there."

"Go right on to Cuzco?"

"Not so foolish as that. Dad wouldn't stand for it. We'll give our island of Cuba so much space that the inhabitants won't even see a speck of us, and we'll make our landing on Jamaica. There's a port called Montego and I'm sure the inhabitants will be delighted to see a couple of little boys who are trying to get along in the world." Bob glanced at the map, did some mental figuring, and nodded his approval.

"We may as well keep our rear seat from knowing what our front seats are doing," he grinned.

"You get brighter by the minute, old man."

"It's the company I keep. I'd be much better if you weren't such a poor skate," Bob retorted.

"Grab your parachute, man, you are going to be dropped into yon briny."

"Unhand me. I say, let's eat in the air. We'll announce that later to Dad. Gosh, he'll think we're bum pilots not being able to see Cuba," Bob chuckled.

"Perhaps he'll take a nap, and I'll tell him you were piloting," Jim announced cheerfully. "Anyway, he'll be glad we are nearer."

"Sure. It's over five hundred miles by a straight line, and we may hit a fog, or a bad wind. Those islands down there are the Keys. See how high you have to get to be out of sight of them." Bob zoomed a thousand feet higher and the tiny dots were lost from their sight.

"That means that an inhabitant, if he has no glasses, can't see us," Jim remarked.

"Yes, but Cuba is three or four hundred miles long and a hundred wide. If we fly straight across it that will take at least twenty minutes, at top speed. Lucky there are no indicators in the passenger seat. You have to remember that Dad's a pilot too," Bob reminded his buddy.

"I don't believe he'd object if he knew. I'll tell him." Jim took up the tube and spoke to his father. "I say Dad, we can make Montego in Jamaica easily before dark. Suppose we do that, then tomorrow we won't have such a long hop."

"Hump. I should be glad to cover the additional miles if you are sure that it isn't going to be too much for you boys and the "Lark". We do not want to be fool-hardy," he answered.

"It'll be easy, and the weather is great. We may as well take advantage of it as long as we can," Jim explained.

"If you are all right when we fly over Cuba, why, go on by all means."

"Good. We'll make a raid on Mom's baskets for supper."

"I'm glad he knows," said Bob, and Jim nodded his agreement.

After that, Austin spent some time observing the ocean rolling by under them, then he got one of his books from under the seat and prepared to do some studying, but he kept the tube in his hand so that his step-brother might call on him without delay. In a few minutes he was so absorbed in what he was learning that he completely forgot he was not at his desk at home or at the laboratory at Don Haurea's. Some time later Bob nudged him, and Jim glanced up.

"Cuba?"

"Must be. I've seen a couple of planes floating around. There's a big fellow over there," Bob remarked and Jim looked in the direction indicated. The long island racing toward them looked remarkably beautiful, and the boy could see numerous boats of all sizes on the water, besides quite a few planes that seemed to be soaring about lazily in the sky as if their owners were merely having a good time.

"Better go higher," Jim suggested. Bob turned the "Lark's" nose into the air, zoomed up swiftly, and raced forward. She was not traveling at the extra speed, so that would not call special attention to her, but while they were still some distance from the island, they saw one plane detach itself from the rest, and start out as if it intended to meet them. It soared swiftly toward them, and Jim watched it thoughtfully, while Bob tried to figure out whether it was merely a friendly advance or someone who was interested in looking them over. He decided not to give the fellow a chance, so he zoomed swiftly up, swerved his course slightly, and sped forward well out of the observer's range of vision. By that time they were nearing Havana, could see the activity of the lovely city, and again Bob climbed, then racing into a cloud bank he put on full speed. Jim watched the other plane, which circled wide before it followed toward the land.

"That guy was looking for us, Buddy, but he doesn't know if it's us, or isn't us," Jim remarked grimly.

"Did I give him the slip?"

"I think so. Can we keep in these clouds?"

"They looked deep when I was watching them," Bob replied grimly.

THE STOWAWAY

The "Lark" soared so high and swiftly over Cuba that it would have taken a racer to have caught even a second glimpse of her, and although it made the trip less simple both boys were glad that the thick atmosphere was not dispelled south of the island. Caldwell grimly made his calculations for their course and Austin checked up on them.

"Methinks this flight is not going to be all baby talk, Buddy," Jim announced.

"Bet my new shirt against a set of red flannels that we hit some hot spots that won't be all Peruvian weather," Bob added.

"Wish we didn't have to stop this side of Belize, but I reckon we better. We're not doing a Lindbergh." Just then the light flashed and Jim took up the speaking tube. "Are you there!"

"Certainly. I observe we are leaving Havana in our rear."

"That's good, we reared right over it and lost the reception committee, if one was out looking for us."

"It's pretty foggy, my boy."

"We don't need to worry about that because we don't have to come down. We'll probably hit some breaks in it before sunset. How do you like the trip? I forgot to suggest that you bring anything to read," Jim laughed, and his father chuckled.

"Mother was more thoughtful. She put in a couple of books— mystery stories, and I have read half of one of them," Mr. Austin answered.

"Great stuff. Maybe we can get some ideas. Got everything you need so that you can eat when the spirit moves?"

"Plenty."

"Because if you haven't, there's a trolley line from the two cock-pits. Just slide up the round disk and you'll find an opening big enough to send a club sandwich through."

"I investigated the disk some hours ago, and I judge it opens behind the passenger seat in front."

"It does. I'll leave the door open so you need not be afraid when it gets dark. Got your sky-light up?"

"No. I find it very comfortable with it down. So long."

"Everything O.K.?" Bob inquired.

"Top hole. He didn't say anything about noticing the plane. He's been reading a mystery story your mother provided."

"That's just like Mom," Bob laughed. Assured that all was well, Jim went back to his studies, and an hour later he looked up at his step-brother, whose expression was a bit tense.

"Let's swap places, old fellow," Jim proposed.

"Don't care if I do." They made the change, and as soon as they were in their places, the younger boy began to investigate the hamper. "Shall I give you a hand out?"

"Sure thing." The fog was considerably more thick than when the plane had dived into it, and as far as Austin could see, there wasn't a break in any direction. He switched on the lights by the control board, but the tiny cabin was bright enough he decided.

"Can you spare a knee?"

"One." Jim moved his leg and Bob spread a napkin, balanced a wooden plate on it, and proceeded to fill it with bread, butter, pickles, cold roast beef, and a bottle of milk. "Go easy," Jim ordered, so the milk was given a safer place on the floor. Although it was early by their watches and also the clock in front of them, they gauged their actions entirely on their stomachs, and attacked the food with keen appetites. When they had eaten all they could, Bob repacked the hamper, then slid his chair forward and prepared to take a nap.

"Better put a coat over you," Jim suggested. He pulled out his own jacket and threw it over his Flying Buddy.

"I say, Jim. Wonder if we hadn't better stick by the plane all night?"

"You mean keep on watch?"

"Yes. We'd be in a dandy fix if we found it with the propeller gone in the morning."

"Let's see what sort of place we can park it in," Jim suggested. He had been wondering uneasily about the town in which they expected to spend the night, and he felt reasonably sure there would be no airdrome, or a garage sufficiently large to admit the plane. On thinking it over, he decided that the island was probably thinly settled, and in that case there must be some sort of barn or open shed. After that, Bob settled back comfortably, his mouth dropped open, and if the engine had not been roaring so melodiously, the boy's snores would have been audible.

"He sure can go to sleep without much trouble," Jim grinned, but he knew that Bob had been so excited the night before that he had slept little, and he had been up two hours earlier than anyone on the K-A that morning. The time passed quickly, and at last the young pilot managed to get above the fog and see the great sun, which was almost setting. He drove along the top of the ceiling for a while, then dived through, and a few miles ahead he made out the dim edge of an island.

"That's Jamaica. It must be," he told himself. Then he picked up the tube to speak to his father in the back. "How goes it?"

"Fine."

"We'll land down here."

"All right. I shall certainly be glad to stretch my legs."

"I say, are we in Peru?" Bob poked up his head.

"We passed that hours ago," Jim laughed.

"Gee, I had a heck of a dream."

"Don't tell it before breakfast, it's bad luck."

Jim circled the "Lark" above the island and selected an open space back of the town which he was sure was Montego. The Jamaica Island lay half hidden in the midst, and the three air travelers sat tensely wondering what the next few minutes would have in store for them. Swiftly the plane glided down and at last lighted near a group of low buildings that might belong to a small piece of farm land. None of them thought it strange that it should be a boy who would come racing inquisitively, for there isn't a youngster on the face of the earth who could resist the force which compels him to run to a descending machine.

"Hello, Bud," Jim called experimentally.

"Hello," the little fellow drawled, and the three were delighted that the salutation was understood.

"May we leave our plane here, and get lodgings for the night?" was the next query.

"Pop's coming." Sure enough, a tall weather-beaten man came leisurely to greet them, and the boy shouted eagerly, "They want to stay the night."

"They kin set in the shed," the man answered.

"Thank you. We'll be glad to pay," Mr. Austin explained.

"Doesn't cost me anything," the man shrugged indifferently.

"It is worth something to us."

"Satisfy yourself. You can get something to eat in the house, but we can't sleep you. There's grass in the shed." With that cordial reception, he strolled off, his son at his heels, and Jim taxied the plane into the long open shed, which might have been built for cows, but had apparently stood unused for months or years. The Flying

Buddies surveyed the place while Mr. Austin made his way to the house to arrange for food. He found a woman with a sick child in her arms, so instead of asking her to prepare a meal, he bought a few supplies which he carried back to the Buddies.

"I didn't get much," he announced.

"We can fix a bunk with the grass," Jim told him. "There's plenty of it and it's clean. We thought we'd sleep down here by the plane, but there's a more comfortable—"

"Let's stay together," the man proposed. "How about gas?"

"We don't have to have it but I may as well see if we can get some in the town. I'll take a walk down and find out. It isn't more than a mile and it's still light enough so that I can find my way," Jim told him.

"Very well. I take it that you think the "Lark" should not be left without a guard."

"Yes, we do, Dad."

"I'll stay with Bob. We can walk around a bit. If we feel like eating there is plenty in the hamper if I didn't get enough from the woman. Have a snack with us before you go?"

"Guess not. I'll trot along."

Jim started across the sandy open space and soon came to a rough winding road that led toward the town. Walking briskly he wished they might stay over a day and get acquainted with that section of the famous island, but perhaps they could do that on the return trip when the business and its dangers were concluded. The boy had gone about half the distance when he overtook a lumbering cart hauled by two young steers, and this struck him as odd. In Canada he had seen ox teams plodding along and had thought them mighty interesting, but the idea of making beasts of burden out of cattle such as ran wild over the vast plains of Texas was a strange sight. As he neared Montego, with its narrow streets and low buildings, he noticed a few people glance after him curiously. Here and there he passed groups of children, ranging in color from fairest little tow-heads, to the blackest and kinkiest. Further along he met an hilarious band dancing mischievously around a hunch-back, who seemed even more dwarfed than his crippledness warranted.

"It's good luck to rub his back," cried one of the tormentors.

"It will make our cow well," put in another as he skipped about the victim in an effort to touch the deformity.

"He keeps witches in his house." Jim eyed the gang resentfully as he drew closer and had made up his mind to interfere, but was saved from participating in the brawl by a tall, military-looking man who suddenly stepped into the midst of the children; brandishing a cane swiftly to right and left.

"Begone, you vagabonds," he shouted, and the youngsters scattered every which way, leaving the crippled dwarf and his rescuer standing alone. Then the man spoke sharply to the hunch-back, who promptly dodged out of sight quite as quickly as if he too expected a blow from the heavy stick. The big fellow looked none too prepossessing, so Austin turned down a near-by lane, and in a few minutes he found himself in what there was of the business section of Montego.

Jim searched about for a sign of a gas-station, but discovered none, then he watched for a garage, either public or private, and at last he came to a small one, where a negro was sleeping contentedly in a backless chair tilted precariously against the wall. The boy glanced into the tumbled building, but there was no sign of filling equipment, and as he stepped by the attendant, the chap opened his eyes a narrow slit.

"I want to buy some gas," Jim told him.

"Yas—"

"Have you got any here?"

"Yas—"

"I'd like to buy some."

"Ebbeyket—" the man drawled, and from the depths of somewhere a second man appeared. He stood a moment eyeing Jim, but the man at the door had resumed his nap.

"I want to buy some gas," Jim explained.

"Yasss—"

"Right away."

The chap yawned, then turned about, and without taking the trouble to make any sort of sign, he shuffled off deeper into the building. Jim followed and hoped the process of purchasing gas was not going to be too complicated. The colored man led the way to the rear, and there, in the dirt floor, Jim saw a deep hole into which one descended by rather a steep incline. The leader of the expedition showed no disposition to go any further.

"Is it down there?"

"Yes." He sat down as if the effort was too much for him.

"How can I get it?" Jim wanted to know. He felt like shaking the fellow, but stuffed his hands into his pockets instead.

"Get it?" Austin couldn't tell whether it was an answer or another question, but he decided to see if he were expected to serve himself, so he started down the narrow incline and in a moment stood before a tumbled door. Through the cave-like opening he saw an odd collection of goods and junk, but in the middle was a familiar metal tank which rested on a pair of saw horses. There was a faucet at one end, and the boy looked around for some sort of container. The only things he could see were some tall empty buckets.

"Haven't you got a covered can?" he called, but the man who had been his escort did not reply, so in exasperation, the boy proceeded to fill one of the pails. He wondered how he would get the stuff to the "Lark," and sincerely hoped that if he had to carry it he wouldn't pass any careless smokers. It took the tiny stream quite a while to fill the pail but finally, when Austin had as much as he wanted, he lugged it up the incline, where he found the colored man curled comfortably on a pile of burlap. He shook the fellow vigorously and finally had him awake.

"Can I get this hauled up the road?" he demanded. The chap shrugged, so the boy went to look for some sort of vehicle and was rewarded by the sight of a team of steers sauntering past the building. "Hey, will you haul some gas up the road for me?" The queer team stopped at the sound of the voice, and the driver turned himself almost all the way around. Jim repeated his question and the man shifted a cud from one side of his mouth to the other.

"I'm through," he remarked indifferently, and the team proceeded on its way, while Jim looked for some other conveyance. He had to go up the street to find one, and as he hurried along he saw the hunchback the children had been tormenting, striding as fast as his short legs would permit, beside the tall man who had scattered the gang. They were an odd pair, and after Austin ran by, the man called quickly, "Looking for someone?"

Jim turned, and the chap smiled cordially.

"I'm getting some gas and want to have it taken to my plane," he explained. "I can't seem to find anyone who isn't asleep." As he spoke, the dwarf faded out of the picture but Jim didn't give him a thought.

"Where is it, the gas, I mean?" the stranger inquired politely.

"In that barn, or whatever it is," Jim answered.

"And your plane?"

"About a mile up the road. We came down back of the town on a sort of farm where we are spending the night."

"I have a small car, I'll fetch it up to you in about an hour, if that will be time enough. I am driving that way," he offered.

"Thank you very much. I'll appreciate it no end," Jim said heartily and wondered why he had thought the man unpleasant.

"It will be no trouble at all. I'm glad to help you out." The chap strode off as if determined not to listen to more thanks, and Jim shook his head.

"I certainly should like to know more about this place. I must have hit it at an odd time, for they are a queer bunch." He went back to the barn, managed to get the doorman to settle the account, and chuckled when the attendant seemed to think that tomorrow would do nicely for the final transaction of the business. Darkness was settling slowly and gently over the land, and Austin started for the camp. He noticed that there wasn't a sign of a star and his trained weather sense warned him that rain was in the air. By the time he reached the point where he had to turn across the field, or whatever it was, it was quite dark, but he saw his Flying Buddy's flash illuminating the shed, and his father's cigar as the man hurried to meet him.

"You were gone quite a while, my boy."

"I guess it takes quite a while to get anything done in Montego, Dad," he laughed, and recounted his experiences to the amusement of his audience.

"At any rate, the man with the car is on the job promptly," Bob announced, as the automobile came tumbling toward them.

"We greatly appreciate—"

"Glad to be able to help you out. I'm on my way to Kingston, and in a hurry." There was something about the brief phrases which did not invite further discussion, so the gas was unloaded quickly and the car dashed off into the darkness.

"Let's get to roost and be on our way at crack of dawn," Bob suggested.

"Suits me," Jim agreed. It had been a long day and he was ready to rest, so he helped the younger boy put the final touches on their bed.

"I'm going to read a little while. You turn in now," said Bob.

"Thought you were going to bed."

"Did intend to, but I guess I'll keep my eyes open."

"Well, all right. You sit with your foot on me and give me a kick if anything goes wrong," Jim directed.

"What's the matter with my sitting the first watch?" Dad proposed.

"Everything. If things aren't all right, I'll call you later."

"Very well." In a few minutes both Jim and his father were sound asleep, while Caldwell doubled up with a book, but he didn't read very attentively. The hours slipped by. Before midnight the world seemed to be enveloped in a mist which was growing thicker, and a bit later, the rain came down in an uncertain sprinkle which gradually grew in strength and courage until it was a downpour. Quietly Bob got rubber blankets, spread one over the sleepers, and wrapped himself in the other. He left his light on, and presently he too was fast asleep. When he opened his eyes the smell of toasting bacon assailed his nostrils and the sight of Jim busy over a camp fire made him sit up quickly.

"Gosh, is it morning?" It was still raining, but the camp was fairly dry, and the breakfast promised to fill a deep cavity.

"It's early, but we're going to start as soon as we can. How late did you sit up?" Jim asked.

"About twelve. Everything all right?"

"Sure. Dad waked about half past twelve and didn't go to sleep again. Then he called me and we decided to let you have a few extra snoozes."

"Thanks." They did not linger over the preparations to get away, and as Mr. Austin had settled with the farmer, there was nothing to detain them, so about the time the sun should have been squinting over the horizon if the weather had been clear, they were in their cock-pits. With the covering in place, they were dry and comfortable, and in the rear, Mr. Austin had tipped his seat to an angle so that he could catch up lost sleep. The "Lark" ran out over the spongy ground, lifted heavily, then went soaring into the air, her motor roaring full blast.

"Well, we got away from there without any trouble," Bob announced with satisfaction as he watched Jim busy with the controls.

"Yes. Reckon we gave that lad at Havana the slip good and proper," he nodded. "Perhaps we were nuts about what he was after, but it was not a bad idea to keep on the safe side. Wow, this is thick."

"All right back there?" Bob called through the tube.

"Quite snug, thank you."

Austin kept the plane climbing steadily until the altitude meter registered twenty thousand feet, then he leveled off for the air was less dense near the ceiling, set his course for Belize, and settled down for the long run to British Honduras. Presently they were soaring through clear skies, but the fog rolled in thick waves and billows beneath them.

"I say, Buddy, change places with me and you can get at those lessons again. I got in some extra licks last night on my stuff," Bob proposed.

"Very well." Presently they had changed places and Austin got out his book and note papers. The plane was sailing smoothly and although the fog reached almost up to them at times, the job of piloting was comparatively easy and the boy thought, with an amused smile, of Don Haurea and his men back in the laboratory.

When he returned home he would see records of the flight, and furthermore, he would probably be able to tell just how dangerous Lieutenant Morrow had been and exactly why that plane in Havana had shown so much interest in their arrival at Cuba. In a short while the boy was completely absorbed in what he was reading and it wasn't until Bob pressed his foot vigorously that his attention was called back to the present.

"I say, there's something rotten about the "Lark". She's been flying rather heavy, and—what in the name of Sampson's donkey is that smell?" Jim glanced at the board and at the same time sniffed cautiously. There was a faint, unfamiliar odor about the tiny cabin, but it was more like the heavy fragrance of too many flowers than anything decaying.

"It's queer. I'll lift the roof." He dropped his work under the seat, unlatched the covering and swung it back. "We haven't needed that thing, and might have put it up when we got out of the rain."

"Yes. Suppose that smell is from tropical plants?"

"Good heavens, how could it be?" Austin picked up the tube to speak with his father, if the man were awake, and as he did so his eyes fell on the reflection globe in which he could see the rear of the plane. The end of the tube dropped from his hand, his lower jaw sagged, and he choked in horror. Bob looked at him quickly.

"What is it, old man?"

"Good God, look." He pointed to the mirror, but the range of Bob's vision was different, so he turned his head. What he saw left him perfectly speechless. All unconscious that he was being observed, some one was crawling out of the rear cock-pit. Someone who looked more like a monkey than a man, and as he clung to the rim, he secured the transparent cover of the cock-pit.

"What is it?" Bob finally gasped.

"The dwarf, Buddy, we didn't get off as easily as we thought."

"That smell must have come through the opening—Jim—your—" But the boy did not finish the sentence.

THE FIGHT IN THE AIR

"My father!" The Sky Buddy's faces paled. "He's been doped back there."

Without a second's hesitation Jim loosened his safety belt, and glanced about for something heavy, but there wasn't a weapon available, so he sprang over the cock-pit, while Bob fought to keep the plane steady. Cold chills of horror were racing up and down his spine, but he kept to his task grimly, twisting around so that he could keep Jim in sight. He did not know who the dwarf was, for in his account of the evening before, his step-brother had said nothing of the pitiful little cripple, but as Caldwell got a look at the sinister figure crouched more like a beast than a human he felt nothing but loathing for the fellow. Vaguely he wondered how the stowaway had gotten there, and what deadly drug had been released in the rear cock-pit.

The force of the wind nearly drove Austin backwards, but he braced himself to keep his balance and clutching the strut, hauled himself along the fuselage. By that time the dwarf had seen the boy coming and with an evil leer, crouched to wait. With a quick lunge Jim reached the rim of the rear cock-pit and glanced through the transparent roofing. He saw his father, not asleep, but slouched low in his seat, his head dropped forward, his hands hanging limp in utter helplessness. With a choking sob the boy dropped, his fingers grabbed the outside latch, and he tugged frantically to lift the cover. For the time being he thought only of getting air to his father; perhaps it was not too late, but every second was precious. With strong fingers Jim managed to shove the latch loose, but before he could do more than that, the dwarf sprang on his back, his long arms entwining around the boy's neck, his legs gripping Jim's thighs. Vainly he tried to shake off the burden, or twist him around, but if the body of the dwarf was crippled, his limbs were amazingly powerful, and the arms as long as a very tall man's. Desperately Jim clawed at the hands, and after seconds of futile effort, he managed to get a grip on the dwarf's thumb and bent it down until he thought the fellow would let it be broken, but at last the assailant was forced to release his hold.

With a quick shake, Austin got free, but only for a moment. He had backed onto the roof of the cabin, and tried to smash it in with his heel, but the material, although frail looking, was a composition made in the Haurea's laboratories and it resisted all his effort as if it were heavy steel. The dwarf sprang again, but Jim ducked under his legs, whirled as he came up, only to meet another furious onslaught, which toppled him backwards. He barely managed to save himself by catching hold of the strut, and the pair swung out over the rolling fog. The "Lark" banked quickly, enabling Jim to get a foothold, and it rode on its side until he was once more standing upright.

Above the roar of the engine, Jim could hear the dwarf bellow in his face, and his hands clawed at the boy's throat. The fellow did not seem to mind whether he remained on the plane or fell off of it, but he was determined to drag Jim with him if he went down. His great fists began to hammer the boy's face and body, but try as he would, Austin was unable to get in an effective blow or do more than defend himself feebly. He realized that Bob at the controls was watching every move, that he made the "Lark" sway, tip, and slant in every direction, but he realized that his Flying Buddy could do little to help him.

Finally a particularly vicious smash sent Jim reeling, his head toward the forward cock-pit, the dwarf on top of him. He caught his victim by the collar and twisted his fingers tightly in the cloth, then his eyes rested on Bob.

"Turn around and go back, or I'll kill him," he shrieked.

"All right. Let go of him and I'll turn around," Bob answered coolly.

"You turn," the fellow roared and his great hand twisted more tightly.

"You win." Caldwell leaned forward over the board; one hand went like a flash downward as the "Lark" began the curve to return. The dwarf glanced out to be sure that the order was being obeyed, then Bob swung up his shoe in his hand, but before he could do anything Jim renewed his struggles and the pair slid over the side into space.

Quick as a flash, Bob tipped the plane's nose downward and followed into the swirling fog. The two dropped swiftly, but in a moment Caldwell saw Austin kick himself free from the clutching arms, sprawl out as he hauled on his parachute, and after a breathless moment, its dark folds opened around the boy's body. Then Bob remembered that the Don had said that in an emergency it would act as a life saver. With the engine racing, the "Lark" cut through the air, dove between the two, partly righted itself and leveled out below Jim. Caldwell stood up as he calculated the distance, and a moment later he felt a thud on the top of the wings as Austin landed, then the pilot reduced the speed until it was barely enough to sustain the plane in the air.

It seemed to the boy as if months passed before he saw Jim's legs slip over the edge of the wing. He watched tensely as his flying buddy climbed painfully down to the fuselage, hung on to the supporting strut, then, the instant he had regained his balance, he hauled the folds of the parachute out of his way and crawled toward the rear cock-pit. In a moment he had the lid up and dropped in beside his father.

"Wow!" Bob glanced at the indicators. They were a thousand up, so he banked around and began to climb as fast as the "Lark" could carry him. He set his lips tightly as he recalled the last he had seen of the dwarf tumbling through the fog toward the ocean below. The fellow had no parachute and the boy wondered why he hadn't taken the precaution to equip himself with one of those in the rear cabin, but it was a mystery he could not answer. Painstakingly Bob studied the map and calculated the course. He had made up his mind to carry on until Jim could let him know how things were in the rear. They were above the fog again, and miles ahead the boy could see the blue waters of the Caribbean Sea stretched beyond the rim of mist. Just then he noticed the light flash over the radio and he picked up the speaking tube. Although he was mighty anxious to hear what his step-brother had to tell him, he dreaded to listen for he was sure that something terrible had happened to his step-father.

"Hello, Old Timer," he tried to call cheerily, but his voice shook.

"Hello yourself. Thanks for the wing-ride. All right up there?"

"Sure thing. Are you battered much?" Bob asked.

"Some, but not enough to put me out," Jim told him.

"How is Dad?"

"Doing fine. Guess when we opened our roof it drove fresh air through that communication tube and that kept him from smothering. Soon as I got this lid open, he came to."

"Oh gosh, I'm glad. Has he told you what happened?"

"He doesn't know. He said that he went to sleep and was dreaming of being choked, and he roused a bit. The air was stinging and his head got full of pains. He tried to signal to us but became unconscious before he could reach the set," Austin explained tensely.

"Do you suppose that kid hid himself back there?"

"Yes. Folded himself in among the luggage. None of us thought to look about either cabin, and when we were up, and Dad asleep, the dwarf let out enough of the stuff he carried to make Dad dopey.

Then he crawled out, smashed the tube and closed the place tight. We had that hole in front open, so it drove some air in; churned it around and we got the stench. That wasn't a kid, it was a man, and whoop, Boy, he did fling a wicked arm. Could you see what happened to him?"

"He didn't have a chute on and while I was trying to get under you, he fell on through the fog," Bob answered.

"Perhaps some fishing boat or vessel will pick him up. Dad says that we must report what happened when we get to Belize."

"Wonder who in blazes he was."

"So do I. I saw him in Montego last night. Funny thing about it, Buddy. Some kids were tormenting him and that lad who brought us the gas chased them off. Later I saw the two of them together, but I didn't think anything about it. Looks serious, Old Timer."

"Sure does. Gosh, I suppose that pig-foot brought him out and told him to stowaway in the plane."

"Expect that's the answer. The dwarf wouldn't have any reason to pick on us. I've got some of the tube and perhaps we can have the stuff analyzed and find out what it is," Jim volunteered.

"He ordered me to turn back. I was going to give him a clip over the head with my shoe, when you slid off taking him with you. Glad you didn't keep such company long."

"I'm right particular about who takes me swimming in the Caribbean."

"Wonder why he didn't get into the extra chute," Bob remarked.

"So do I, but I guess he was hiding under it. After this we shake the "Lark" out before we leave. Got anything to eat?"

"Sure. Shall I send some through to you?"

"No. There's enough. After a while I'll crawl forward and relieve you, Old Timer. Much obliged for the cooperation."

"Always glad to oblige. I say, it seems queer to me that a man should take such a chance. If you saw them together, the fellow should have known you'd connect him with the slaughter."

"Maybe, Bob, but I expect he planned we'd all go merrily down to Davie's locker and it wouldn't make a particle of difference what we had seen or suspected. I didn't get the details of the plot from my late opponent but if I ever meet him again, you bet I will. So long." The tube was hung up and Bob, with a mighty thankful heart attended to his job. He managed to get something to eat out of the hamper, and occasionally he'd wave an arm to his fellow travelers. Presently Mr. Austin was sitting up straight, apparently none the worse for his experience, and he smiled cheerily to his step-son.

Half an hour later the plane was sailing swiftly through clear skies, and before noon the rugged outline of the long coast of the Central American countries rose mistily out of the depths. It was a welcome sight to the flyers, and when the sun was almost straight above their heads, beating furiously, Bob started to glide to land and in a little while he had dropped onto a British field. Several English soldiers started toward them, and an officer came forward to speak to them.

"What's this, a non-stop flight?" the man smiled.

"No, sir. We've made a couple of stops since we left Texas."

"My name's Seaman. Anything I can do for you?"

"Mine's Austin." He introduced himself and the Flying Buddies explained briefly why they had dropped out of the sky.

"Won't you join us for lunch?" Seaman invited cordially. "We're always delighted to have visitors."

"Thank you. We shall be happy to join you. There is something which I must report and no doubt you can tell me just where to do it."

"It will give me great pleasure." The officer led the way to the barracks and his own quarters. "Make yourselves as comfortable as the heat will permit." The three washed up, and then, seated under a whizzing fan, Mr. Austin told him about the stowaway. The man's eyes were raised incredulously, but there was no doubting the story.

"You say that you are on a business trip; to Peru?"

"Yes. An important one."

"No doubt someone, or group, is interested in seeing that you don't get there," Seaman suggested.

"That must be the solution, but it is very mystifying for we did not decide to fly down until two days before we started, and only a few close friends and the family knew how we were making the trip," Mr. Austin told him.

"You are quite safe here, and we'll do anything we can for you. I'll make a report of your story, have it written this afternoon, and if you'll sign it before you leave, it will be on record in case anything should come up later. If that dwarf is picked up by a boat he may claim that he was thrown out of the plane and make things unpleasant in that way. I'll give you a copy of the papers with our signatures, and you can keep it on you to use if need be."

"I have a part of the tube," Jim explained.

"Leave a few drops of the stuff here and we'll analyze it. See if our chemists can recognize the drug. There are hundreds of varieties picked up in the jungles every once in a while, but I never happened to hear of one acting as this did. You're lucky to be here."

"We certainly do appreciate your assistance," Mr. Austin said warmly.

"I'll have a guard posted by your plane while it is here so there will be no possible chance for a recurrence of what happened this morning, and when you are ready to refuel you can supervise the business yourselves. We have some good mechanics if you need any work done," he offered further.

"We'll give the bird an examination and be mighty glad to have your man's help if anything has to be done," Jim told him. Seaman touched a button and in a moment an orderly appeared. He stopped just inside the door, saluted briskly.

"Send in the clerk, and give orders that the American plane is to be carefully watched—strictly. No one, other than the guard, to go near it, except the flyers, of course."

"Very well, sir." The man touched his cap again, wheeled and went out briskly. The officer turned again to his guests.

"Did you mention a ranch, the K-A?"

"That's ours," Bob said quickly. "The K-A and the Cross-Bar; they're great ranches."

"I do not doubt it. I have a friend, an old school pal who is one of the Royal Mounted Police Chiefs stationed in Quebec. A few weeks ago I received a letter from him and he told me that he had been in Texas on some official business. As I recall it, he said he stayed at the K-A, and he mentioned some rather wild experiences at another place—"

"The Box-Z," Jim laughed.

"That's it. Chap's name is Allen Ruhel."

"He stopped with us. We met him first in the Province of Quebec, and another chap, named Bradshaw. We had some great times in Canada, near the line, and we told them if they came to Texas we'd pin horseshoes on them, but they didn't stay long enough," Bob announced.

"By George, then you are the Flying Buddies he spoke of. Said most disrespectfully that a couple of "American kids" had done a lot to locate the hangout of a border gang. He's particularly grateful to you because it proved to his department that planes can be of the greatest assistance in the work to be done, and he's getting some extra ones in his service," Seaman smiled. "You did him quite a good turn."

"Howling Nightingales, they did us a few," Bob declared.

"Being pals, Allen and I pass on bits of information which may come in handy in our work. He told me that there was a grand round-up of criminals at that ranch in Texas, but he also said that two men, the son of one of the leaders and their chauffeur managed to escape the net. Do you happen to know if the man has been captured?"

"He wasn't a couple of days ago. That's Arthur Gordon. The sheriff at Crofton had the old ranch guarded by a young deputy. We had to stop there one day before Christmas, and discovered that Gordon was there, but he saw us first," Jim explained.

"Which means that he got in some dirty work and made his get away."

"He surely did." Bob told the story briefly, not leaving out anything and with casual references to Don Haurea, and Seaman was greatly interested.

"He's a bad boy all right-o. What do you suppose he wanted with carrier pigeons?"

"He must use them to send communication to some long-distance point."

"Yes, of course. It will be well to remember that he has a supply and notify the authorities to be on the watch for them. A plane can trail one easily if it is once spotted. It seems strange that Gordon abandoned your airplane."

"That occurred to us, but we're glad he did," Bob grinned.

"Who wouldn't be!"

"Probably the young fellow had another means of leaving the State or the country. He may even have had a plane of his own, and of course he would know that a description of your machine would be well broadcasted. He didn't have gas enough to get very far, so he dropped out where he knew he would find friends and either hid until the matter blew over somewhat, or left immediately," Mr. Austin volunteered.

"Very true." Just then the clerk appeared with pad and pencil, and Seaman dictated briefly the story of the dwarf's attempt to suffocate the air travelers and his probable fate. The clerk took it on the typewriter, and when it was finished the Texans and the two Britishers signed it in triplicate.

"You keep this copy in your possession." Seaman handed one sheet to Mr. Austin, who put it with his papers in his pocket.

"Thank you very much."

"Now, we may as well have lunch." He led the way to the mess hall where a number of officers were assembled, introduced his companions, and the three sat down at one of the small tables. The meal was a lively affair, the men joked back and forth, some of the older ones told stories, and when they had finished, the two grown-ups lighted cigars.

"You do not have such a dull time," Mr. Austin remarked.

"No, indeed," Seaman smiled, then he added gravely, "I have a suggestion to make. By air it's in the neighborhood of three thousand miles to Cuzco from here. Lay to quietly today, get your crate in order, and start tomorrow morning about three o'clock, then make it a non-stop. That will put the kibosh on any plan to get you between here and your destination. It is possible that I'll get some word by wireless if the dwarf is picked up, but from what you say of your position at the time, the fellow was a bit out of the track of usual travel. However, boats do go roaming about all over the sea, and one might have been on the spot."

"I thought he might have planned to drop off where someone was waiting for him," Jim suggested.

"That's possible. Also, he may have been sure that he could force you to turn back to Jamaica. That would explain the fact that he was not prepared for a fall into the sea. Too bad his backer didn't take the drop with him. You say you have some reliable friends who are associated with you in this business. I might get a message through to expect you tomorrow afternoon some time if you care to have me."

"I think it is an excellent plan," Mr. Austin answered. "How about it, boys?"

"Suits me," Jim answered.

"I haven't a single amendment to offer," Bob added.

"Very well. Then make yourselves at home, get all the rest you can before you start. I'm mighty glad you dropped in on me, and when I write Allen, I shall take pleasure in telling him that I have met The Flying Buddies."

AT CUZCO

As far as Seaman could learn no wireless message was picked up regarding the fate of the dwarf, but the officer promised the Texans that he would notify them if he got any information.

"I doubt very much if the fellow is alive but some people are born lucky; you never can tell what they will come through. A decent man hitting the water from that distance would have the life knocked right out of him and sink like lead to the bottom. We have your description of the pair, so I'll send out some quiet inquiries. I'd like to pick up that man who hauled your gas for you at Montego."

"Hope you do," Jim said earnestly.

"We may. It's amazing how that sort of riffraff drifts about. Well, now, you fellows turn in. The guard will call you in time to start, and if you are ever in the neighborhood again, pay us another call."

"Sure, we will. Perhaps when we're coming back we'll have time to spend a day and see this part of the world. It sure looks interesting; something like the level parts of Texas," said Bob.

"You are a confirmed Texan," Seaman smiled as he withdrew, and presently the weary travelers had drifted off into the land of dreams, and not even the heat disturbed them. When the guard finally knocked softly at the door to let them know it was time to get up, the air was chilly, and they yawned vigorously.

"Captain Seaman said to tell you that our chemist couldn't find out what was in that broken tube. He applied all the tests we have, but it's something he doesn't know anything about," the man explained.

"Thank you very much."

"He sealed the rest in a container because he thought you might like to keep it, or send it to another analyst." The soldier produced a tube and Jim took it thoughtfully.

"Could you send it by air mail for us from here?"

"Yes sir, certainly."

"I'm going to send it to the Don, Dad. Perhaps he can have it analyzed by some one."

"That's a good plan. Anyway, it will be well to preserve it."

Jim took a few minutes to get the tube ready to mail, then dressed quickly, and joined his father and buddy, who were already being served a good breakfast in the great empty mess-hall. Before they had finished, Captain Seaman appeared in his pajamas and bathrobe.

"Rest well?" he asked.

"Never better. Sorry to get you out at such an ungodly hour."

"That's all right. I thought I'd like to see you off safely so I told the guard to call me." He sat down and chatted with them until they had finished, then went to the "Lark" about which a sentry marched in perfect military fashion and very businesslike. He saluted the captain, seemed relieved at the sight of the travelers, and stood respectfully while the party prepared to leave.

"We owe you a great deal, Captain Seaman," Mr. Austin declared holding out his hand.

"Glad we could do anything for you."

The three climbed into their places, Jim at the controls, and in a moment the engine was roaring. Except for the camp lights, the night was pitch black but they all knew that the dawn would be breaking before very long. The travelers and the soldiers waved farewells, then the "Lark" gave a gay little hop, and raced into the air. She seemed to realize that she had a great deal to do before she came down again, so she set to work with a good will. Jim climbed her thirty thousand feet before he leveled out, set his course, and shot forward like a star through the blackness. Twice Bob called through the speaking tube to the passenger in the rear, and Mr. Austin assured them he was quite safe and comfortable.

"I find that by sitting low my hands come close to the bulb, my boy, so that I can signal you the instant I scent danger, and as long as I can catch an occasional glimpse of your heads I am assured that all is well up front," he told them.

"Corking idea. Do you see that morning star? Isn't she a beauty?"

"She certainly is magnificent, but she will not shine very much longer for I believe that I see a sign of light in the distance." After that chat they flew in silence, then Bob set himself to studying, while Jim continued to keep to his task of piloting. It seemed to him that Captain Seaman's suggestion to continue the trip without a break was a very sensible one, and as he considered the matter he thought that Panama, where they had intended to make a stop might have proved another unlucky spot for them. There was no doubt now that someone was making a strenuous effort to prevent them from reaching Cuzco, and whoever was organizing the movement against them would have given Belize small consideration.

An hour later daylight was well on its way and the morning was glorious. The sun rose like a brilliant ball of color which reflected in numberless dancing shades on the vast expanse of water that was so much greater in proportion than the bits of land it surrounded. The "Lark" was going at top speed and never did the boys see the world roll under them so swiftly. It hardly seemed possible that an airplane could fly so fast, but the miles were clicking off on the indicator and the wind screamed sharply as they cut through it. Austin wondered if anything would happen that would necessitate carrying them along by the force of the central power and then he recalled that Don Haurea had said that one of the stations was in South America. The "Lark" must even now be in touch with it and the boy wished he had remembered to ask exactly where it was located. Staring ahead toward the distant land to which he was going he thought again of those ancient Spaniards and he tried to visualize the years that had passed, if the intellect of those adventurers would have been as highly developed as their brute courage. Into his mind came the recollection of the bitterness in the voice of the dignified Don when he spoke of the Pizarros, then through it flashed a vague idea. He wondered if the Haureas were descendants of those Yncas. It made him gasp.

Almost immediately came the recollection of that day in Vermont when he and Bob had gone to the little island in Lake Champlain to find Corso and his young nephew. How they had found the boy garbed in the exquisite robes of royalty, and how they had listened as Yncicea had told them of the ancient race which had preserved itself through the centuries. The youngster looked every inch a prince as he made his explanation simply, the chest of precious jewels at his feet. As a token of appreciation the Flying Buddies had each received two very valuable emeralds beside the rings they wore on their fingers.

"What a blue-ribbon turnip I've been. Yncicea is Don Haurea's son. Ynca—that's part of the title of the children of The Sun. Great Scott, of course—they are descendants of the Yncas—the real ones. Well, gosh, I'm glad of it. It'll take more than a bunch of ignoramuses to ride rough shod over them again. Gee, I wonder how many there are now; some tribe, I'll bet—"

"Talking in your sleep?" Bob demanded. He had happened to look up and saw Jim's lips moving.

"I just had a great idea."

"Cherish it, Old Timer, you may never get another," Bob taunted.

"I shall," Jim chuckled. Caldwell returned to his notes while Jim's mind was filled with the wildest fancies. He was mighty glad that Her Highness had come down on the Box-Z that day when they were out of gas. It seemed as if it must have occurred years instead of months ago. So much had happened; so much that was thrilling; and so much that was perfectly fascinating. The possibilities for the future had opened out swiftly, there seemed to be no limit to what could be accomplished. Toward the middle of the morning Bob looked up again.

"Remember when we ate?"

"Haven't the faintest recollection," Jim admitted. The younger boy put away his work and attacked the hamper. He called to Mr. Austin, who declared that all was well with him.

"I have a book, a sandwich, a piece of cake and a bottle of coffee right this minute," he announced.

"You're getting ahead of us," Bob laughed. Presently he had eaten all he wanted, then he turned to Jim. "Now, bring that idea of yours over here and don't eat so much, you'll crowd it out."

"Don't you worry, I hog-tied it," Jim retorted. They changed seats and Austin looked into the basket. "You ate it all," he bellowed.

"Did not, there's half a chicken and all the trimmings," Bob grinned. "Maybe so much brain work has affected your eyesight." Austin produced the chicken and trimmings and set to work on them, then, after a chat with his father, he got at his books. The "Lark" soared along steadily, smooth as silk. They were over the Andes now and as Caldwell glanced at them his mouth opened in awe and wonder. He hoped hard that the business which was bringing them would not be concluded too quickly for he longed to fly over those long-jagged ridges, to explore their dark forests and follow some of those rushing streams that glistened in the valleys. Far away the boy could see the edge of the Pacific Ocean. Occasionally he caught a glimpse of a great ship, then he saw numberless small boats bobbing on the waves. Although he scanned the air for a plane no one seemed to be flying, and he wondered at that, for he was sure that pilots would be crazy about the land. Along the coast were numerous towns, inland they were more scattered, and they seemed to be perched on the mountain sides. Further south began the deserts, arid and barren, their hot shifting sands looking exactly like set waves.

"We ought to be almost there, Buddy," Jim remarked as he looked up from his work and glanced at the chart. "That must be Lima beyond us. Suppose you shoot over east a bit."

"All right." Bob changed the course and turned the plane's nose in toward the mountains.

"Want to change?"

"Don't care if I do. The sun has been kind of glaring." They shifted places again and Caldwell heaved a sigh of relief.

"Why didn't you tell me that you were getting fagged?"

"Didn't think of it. This surely is some country." They drove on swiftly, and finally Mr. Austin flashed the signal.

"My friend's home is east of the city. He wrote me that one of his neighbors has a plane, so there must be a landing space near by."

"We'll look for it, Dad." By that time the mountain city and the great lake Titicaca came into view. Bob pulled down his cap glasses and did some close observing, and finally he pointed out a place which should be convenient for landing. It was after two o'clock when they brought the "Lark" down on a broad field which looked as if it were a part of a plantation. They waited a few minutes to glance around, and presently a young man came striding toward them.

"May I serve you gentlemen?" he asked politely.

"Are we near the Pedro De Castro place?" Mr. Austin inquired.

"You are on it, sir. The house is on the terrace. You can taxi your plane quite close. The avenues are wide enough so that you can drive over them easily."

"Thank you very much." Jim started the last lap of the trip, and he wondered if anything could possibly happen now to prevent the proper promotion of the business to be settled. They had barely swung around toward the house, when he saw a tall man come quickly from the veranda and hurry to meet them.

"Gentlemen, gentlemen, this is a pleasure. I received word that you were on your way but I calculated that you could not possibly reach here before evening. You must have a very good plane and pilot." He was a dark-eyed and pleasant faced chap and he went at once to the rear cock-pit where he and Mr. Austin shook hands cordially. "Alight at once. It is an inactive time of day. Do come and make yourselves comfortable."

"You must meet the boys. My son Jim and Bob Caldwell."

"Did I not meet this one years ago, and do I not remember his tow-head, but he has forgotten me I am sure. Run your bus in the shade, boys, and come into the house. You can care for it later." He shook hands all round, and the boys grinned uneasily, but soon they were inside, where they were introduced to Carlos, dark-eyed like his father, but his hair was brown and he was nearly sixteen years old.

"I wish you would tell me at once about this business, Peter. I am anxious to know what has been happening," Mr. Austin urged.

"Come into the gardens. May I bring my son? He is getting to be a man and he must begin to learn things."

"By all means. I've been shifting responsibilities on the shoulders of my boys and while they do not know much about this project, I should be glad to have them sit in. We old fellows never know when we may have to leave the reins in younger hands and I think it wrong not to let them have as much experience as possible." They made their way to a beautiful portico which reminded the Sky Buddies of Don Haurea's home, only this was much more pretentious. Comfortable seats were placed, and when they were settled a servant came with cool drinks in iced glasses.

"You were wise to come, Austin. I felt sure that I could depend upon your co-operation, and now that you are here we can conclude the matter without delay," De Castro told them.

"That is good. What has been going wrong?"

"More than we thought. You know that much of the management has been left in the hands of Vaca Alonzo and his brother, Silvester. While the work was being developed they both devoted themselves to it tirelessly, then I noticed a change in Silvester, he seemed less open and responsive. He is the older man. One or two others in the company mentioned several slight discrepancies, so we started a quiet investigation. We found that they are maneuvering to gain control of the business. Several outsiders have been admitted, one at a time, unobtrusively, and these men have been making an effort to increase their stock. You understand the sort of thing that can be—as you say in the United States—put over, when the heads of an organization are not alert?"

"Yes, indeed," Mr. Austin answered.

"Well, you are here, two other men will arrive later, one is already on his way from Lima. At the regular meeting tonight we will out-vote them, and under the circumstances I am in favor of changing officers, giving the Alonzos less influence. It is good that you arrived so promptly for we had planned to seek an adjournment tonight, but that will not be necessary. We can conclude the matter immediately, and it is possible that we can rid ourselves of the undesirable element."

"I am certainly in favor of that," Mr. Austin declared. "Now, I should like to ask you something. Are the Alonzos very widely connected?"

"Why yes, they are, I should say. They have interests in several enterprises. That is one reason why we wanted them to join with us. While they were not what you would call enormously wealthy, they have been very successful in the past two years. May I ask why you inquire?"

"Your letter by air mail reached me in good time and we started within the week, as you know. We have made the trip in excellent time and as far as we can tell you, only our immediate families were aware we were coming here to Cuzco. I did not even send you a message because it occurred to me that someone might investigate your mail."

"When I did not hear from you, I felt positive that you were coming," De Castro smiled.

"That's what I expected you to do. Texas, our part of it, has been under a blanket of snow for several weeks, so we have seen little of our neighbors, and I doubt if any of them know that we are not at home," Mr. Austin explained carefully.

"Yes, it is well to be cautious; there is much at stake."

"To shorten the story, one attempt was made on my life, possibly two, but the one came very nearly being accomplished. I wondered if the Alonzos are sufficiently powerful to have an organization which could be responsible for those attempts."

"Humph. Well, I believe they are. And, since you mention it, two of our important directors were mysteriously ill at the time of the last meeting. They recovered in a day or so, but their medical men are still at a loss to know what was the matter with them. They have been taking every precaution since, in fact, they have had themselves and their homes strictly guarded," De Castro announced, then added, "But there is no one they suspect, and as far as I know, there seems to have been no way to connect their illness with the Alonzos."

"But the fact that the men were ill is in itself suspicious."

"I should say that it is, very. May I ask what happened on your way here, and how you escaped?"

"I escaped because of my son's promptness in acting, and Bob's co-operation." Mr. Austin went on to tell the story since the arrival at Miami where the supposed Marine tried so hard to be taken to Havana, and the discovering of the dwarf after he had attempted to drug the flyers. The De Castros listened tensely during the recital, and at its close, the older man got to his feet and paced up and down in his agitation.

"Barbarous, simply barbarous. The assassins. You say the chemist was unable to classify the drug?"

"He didn't know it. We sent the tube north and hope to get it analyzed, but he had no idea what it contained."

"Great guns, you boys must have had a wild time fighting that dwarf," Carlos exclaimed.

"Jim did the fighting. I was frozen to the controls," Bob answered.

"Sure he was, but I'd have gone into the briny with a bumped head if he hadn't kept the "Lark" doing stunts. When we did slide off, he dove down under me so that I dropped on top of the wings. They sure did look good to me," Jim declared.

"You didn't look around for the dwarf?"

"As soon as a chute opens a man begins to fall slowly, and if he has his wits about him, he can guide himself in any direction. I knew that when Jim saw the plane coming under him, he'd make for it even if I didn't get in exactly the right position. We were in a fog, and the dwarf just went tumbling on, going faster and faster. He was out of sight before I had picked up Buddy, then we were getting pretty low, so I began to climb. I didn't know anything about what the water was like, so I didn't dare go down. I might have landed on it half a mile from where the dwarf dropped," Bob told them simply.

"And with the force the fellow would keep dropping."

"Yes."

"Well, my boys, you tell it as if it were a mere incident, but I know those were anxious moments for you all—ah, here are our two associates. Now, I am sure that we shall have things in our own hands and that all will be well after the meeting. Carlos, do take the boys where they can rest, and tomorrow perhaps you can show them something of our land. We think it very marvelous."

"I say, maybe they'd like to fly to Amy-Ran. That's mighty interesting and I've always wanted to get there in a plane. It's an old Indian place, I won't tell you anything about it, you can see for yourself. No one ever goes near it much, but there's an Indian woman, no one knows how old she is, who lives near by," Carlos told them.

"That surely sounds as if it would be worth seeing," the Buddies agreed heartily. "Suppose you'll be staying over tomorrow, Dad?"

"I believe that I may have to," Mr. Austin answered.

"Stay over the day! Indeed you are, you shall stay several days," De Castro announced emphatically.

AMY-RAN FASTNESS

The meeting that evening at De Castro's became, before its close, what the Flying Buddies and Carlos termed a "hot session." It was held in one of the huge cool rooms and the three young fellows stationed themselves on a balcony which gave them an excellent view without revealing their presence. The Alonzos and their faction arrived promptly, were greeted with great politeness by a young man secretary, and took their places around the heavy table with expressions of grave importance. To Jim, the younger man seemed to squirm a bit uneasily in his chair but every other face registered imperturbability. However, there were hastily exchanged glances when a second group of three men entered, but their appearance seemed to cause no special alarm. Courteous pleasantries were passed back and forth as all were seated. Eight men were assembled, there was no show of impatience, but an occasional glance toward the door through which they expected the elder De Castro to enter. The secretary had arranged a neat pile of notes and books at the head of the table, where was the only empty chair. Then the portieres, rustled slightly, the tall Peruvian stepped forward, with Mr. Austin and two other gentlemen beside him.

As if they had suddenly discovered something extremely hot on their seats, the Alonzos sprang to their feet, but they promptly recovered their poise and concealed their chagrin with effusive welcomes. Soon the meeting was called to order, more chairs brought in, and preliminaries started.

"Looks like a disarmament conference," Bob whispered, and his buddy nodded assent. The Texans were watching with cool interest, but Carlos was quivering with excitement.

"They may try to do harm to my father," he said softly.

"We'll keep an eye on them," Jim promised firmly. He realized that Carlos was more familiar with the details of the business and that his anxiety was probably warranted. They watched the meeting proceed, could see the strained tension as more and more important matters were brought up, and finally heard the younger Alonzo burst out angrily.

"He is declaring that there is an attempt to—what you call—deposit two crosses on him." Jim frowned, then smothered a chuckle as he understood the boy meant "double cross."

"Perhaps he'll find, before the evening is over, that he's been branded with a flock of crosses," Austin answered.

"Let us hope so." After that there was a heated discussion. De Castro and his side remained calm, and finally, when a vote was taken, it was discovered that two of the opposition had changed their tactics and were uniting themselves with the stronger, safer side. That infuriated both Alonzos and three of their men, but when they saw that four servants who entered unostentatiously with trays and glasses, were powerfully built fellows, they lowered their voices and sat back in their seats.

"They understand now they are in for a revelation of their hands," and Bob guessed that meant a "show-down." Carlos was correct. Because of the presence of Mr. Austin and the other two, detailed questions were taken up, books examined with great care, and matters gone into very thoroughly. There was an attempt to hedge, a postponement proposed, but Jim's father quietly announced that he wished the business concluded at once. He was ably backed, so they went on, and finally, the election of officers began. At the count it was found that the Alonzos were out of power. That started a violent harangue, accusations true and false, and so many pairs of fists hammered the great table that it jumped as if spooks were under it. Politeness was thrown to the winds, and it was hard for the three boys on the balcony to keep quiet. They longed to leap in and take a part in the fray, but restrained themselves manfully, for Mr. Austin had told Jim that they must not interfere unless there was actual danger. At last it was over, the meeting was closed, and five of the assembly left the place with faces which were black with anger, and feet that stamped heavily all the way down the terrace to their waiting cars. Then Carlos threw open the door, and the fathers smiled at their sons' eagerness.

"You got away with it, didn't you, Dad!"

"We did, my boy. I almost forgot that you were out there. What do you think of business meetings?"

"This one looked to me like a warm party. Do you believe that those fellows are responsible for the attacks on you?"

"Yes, I do. Before they knew that I was here, they telephoned Mr. De Castro urging that everything be taken up tonight. That pleased us greatly, and when we came into the room, the pair of them looked at me as if they thought I were a ghost. They thought they had everything their own way and it maddened them to be taken so by surprise," he answered.

"We turned on them the surprise elements of the meeting," Mr. De Castro smiled, then added, "You boys are not aware that it is nearly morning and time young heads were on pillows."

"I'm happy that it is over, my father, but I am sure that you will need to be cautious. The Alonzos are not going to take kindly to their defeat," Carlos declared solemnly. He kissed his father quite naturally, to the surprise of the Texas boys, then Jim remembered that these people were more demonstrative than in northern countries. Not to be outdone he kissed his own father, and Mr. Austin accepted the salute, then turned and embraced Bob.

"Frolicking frogs, but I'm glad you could get here," Caldwell declared, and didn't even flush at the demonstration.

"I am particularly grateful to you two for getting me here. Now, as Peter says, it is time heads, both young and not so young, were on pillows," Mr. Austin told them.

"Shall we stay over tomorrow?" Jim wanted to know.

"I think probably it will be necessary for me to stay several days, my boy. Things we took up tonight need to be carried through and I should not care to leave all the responsibility to my friends."

"That is splendid. We shall pay the visit to Amy-Ran," Carlos declared with delight. "It will be a pleasure to show you something which is magnificent." It did not take long for the household to quiet down for the balance of the night. Before they finally turned in, Bob was frowning seriously.

"I say, Buddy, Carlos seemed to think that his father may have a mess on his hands with those fellows. They must be just as sore at Dad," he said finally.

"Reckon they are, but I heard Dad and Mr. De Castro discussing that this afternoon and they agreed that if the Alonzos failed to put through their scheme they will be mighty careful. They are influential men, that is, I mean prominent in a number of ways, and if it came out that they tried to put over something underhanded, they would all be ruined. There is plenty of evidence against them so that anything that went wrong could be pinned on them hard and fast," Jim explained.

"I see. Then they'll be more likely to do, their utmost to see that nothing serious happens," Bob remarked.

"Exactly. Dad and Mr. De Castro have them where they want them. They are hog-tied good and plenty."

"Fine. Good-night." The Flying Buddies went to sleep with contented minds, satisfied that the job they had undertaken was well done. It was late when they awoke, but the household was stirring quietly, and the De Castro family were radiant over the successful outcome of the meeting. As soon as they could get on their way, the three boys set out for Amy-Ran, young Carlos in the seat with Jim and Bob in the rear cock-pit where he crowed over his step-brother because he could observe without interruption the world over which they would travel.

"You'll have to pilot the return trip," Jim declared.

"Suits me," the young fellow laughed. Carlos had a map of the country and pointed out the section of the mountains to which they were going, and presently the "Lark" was soaring gracefully over the city. The course was set and the Texans both thrilled with wonder at the beauty of the Andes rolling under them. It took half an hour to reach the point and Carlos shouted they had gone far enough, then Jim circled again, picked out a flat stretch of high table land and glided down. The plane lighted easily, the three climbed out, and the Sky Buddies gasped in awe at the magnificence of their surroundings, while young De Castro smiled with gratification at their admiration.

"This is almost inaccessible from below," he announced. "Only a few white people have ever been able to get up here."

The place where they stood was about half an acre wide, seemed to be of solid rock, which ended abruptly a few rods ahead, and as they had landed, Bob had noticed that the sides were perpendicular and seemed to drop in jagged formation at least a thousand feet. From the elevation they got a gorgeous view of sharp cliffs, lower hills, the plain, and finally the sea stretching into the horizon. Behind them was a small lake, which lay like a glittering blue jewel in a deep bowl. The plateau was in the shape of an S, and after they had stood staring some time at the scene, Carlos touched Jim's arm.

"We shall leave the plane here and I'll show you something more astounding than this."

"Hadn't we better block the bird?" Bob suggested, but there were neither logs nor rocks available.

"I'll raise the wheels and let her rest on the floats. They clutch the surface like a tire and if it should blow up much we'll have to get away quickly," Jim decided. Presently that was accomplished, then Carlos led them cautiously along the narrow S until at last they were near the further end where they paused again.

"Gee, look at these sentinels. Don't they look like something built up here," Bob exclaimed as he saw a giant rim of smooth stones which rose like a wall close by them.

"They were brought here, but no one knows how," Carlos told them.

"How do you know they were brought here?" Bob demanded.

"When you examine them you can see that the rock is much different from any around this part of the country, and also you can see that they were set in, like a foundation. There is a story that the conquerors who came here found an unfinished temple. The stones are fine quality, such as the ancient temples to the Sun God were made of, but these were so firmly planted and high up, that they could not be hauled down or destroyed. Where they could, the conquerors wrecked the temples and used the stones in their own buildings but some of the walls of the temple of Lake Titicaca are still standing. There isn't a crack in them where they were joined," Carlos replied.

"Must be a great piece of work," Bob remarked.

"It is and no one knows how it was done. So many of the Indians were killed that their amazing skill was lost in a few years."

"Some of them were fine jewelers—they knew a lot of things—I've read about Lake Titicaca and the temple there," Jim said quietly.

"There is a difference of opinion as to whether that was the emerald temple, or this place here. Once when I was a little fellow I came up with some other boys, but we didn't hang around very long. We had to do some dangerous climbing, throw ropes ahead and haul ourselves that way. The land hereabouts belongs to what is left of one of the tribes and cannot be taken away from them, but as far as I have ever heard, only one very old Indian woman is ever around. A funny thing happened the time I came, I was scared out of my wits, and I went along that wall pressed as close as I could get because I was sure that I'd fall. I felt one of the stones move and it slid open. When I reached my companions I told them about it and we all came back but I couldn't find the place. They laughed at me, of course, but just the same I'm positive it moved."

"Remember where it was?" Jim asked.

"Perhaps we can move it," Bob added. Carlos led the way he had taken as a youngster but although they pressed hard all the way, every section remained firm and unmoved as the mountains themselves.

"Everybody has told me that it was my terrified fancy and I suppose it was, but I'm not gifted with a very lively imagination," Carlos said.

"When it was open what did it look like?" Bob inquired.

"It only opened a little way and all I could see was a flat place beyond with some flowers. I raced off to get the other boys, then couldn't find it. Come along further and see the different parts." He led the way and soon they were walking through a series of unfinished sections, some roofed and others open to the sky. The stone of the mountain formed the natural flooring, but here and there were huge inlaid pieces which still bore strange markings. On some of the stones were designs so weather-beaten that they could not be made out, and quite a number of them were highly colored.

Suddenly they heard a soft sound behind them, and whirling quickly they were confronted by a very tall woman whose dark face was as wrinkled as a black walnut, and whose hands rested on the gnarled head of a heavy stick. She stood perfectly quiet, her eyes traveling from the top of Carlos' head to the tips of his toes, then she turned her gaze on the two Texans. Bob felt the hair on his back chill as if he were leaning against a block of ice, but Jim had no fear under the close scrutiny.

"Put forward your hands, all of you," she ordered, and they obeyed. The two emerald rings on the fingers of the Flying Buddies gleamed in the sunlight. She glanced from one to the other, then into their faces. "Go in peace," she said, then turned about and disappeared behind a partition. Carlos whistled softly.

"Guess we'd better not stay around," he remarked firmly. Jim and Bob exchanged glances.

"I do not believe that she will mind our looking at the place if we are careful not to disturb anything," Bob suggested because by that time he was sure there was nothing to be afraid of and he very much wanted to inspect the marvelous monument that stood so sturdily as a reminder of its clever builders.

"We'll be mighty careful," Jim added, but as they walked forth, Carlos was no longer leading. He was perfectly contented to follow, and although he glanced hither and yon, they did not see the ancient guardian again. It took some little time to tour the whole place and finally they came to the end where they stopped to catch their breaths.

"Whew, it's like something one reads about," Bob declared softly. "This high ledge dropping straight down to goodness knows where, and this wild S-plateau studded with spires of the Andes. No wonder the original owners have been allowed to remain in possession. A white man couldn't do a blame thing with the place."

"I suppose that tourists and mountain climbers come up occasionally," Jim added.

"Very few. Some years ago there was a half-breed guide who used to bring people. He had rigged a sort of basket and ropes out of fibre, very strong, but two parties were killed because the stuff rubbed on the sharp rocks and broke. The last time, the guide himself took a header into the canyon, and since then everybody gives Amy-Ran a wide birth. As it does not belong to the province of Peru, the government forbade travelers visiting it. Only once in a while a few boys will climb up, but I remember when I came it was even harder to get down than up, and I had no inclination to make a second attempt. When I saw the plane I thought it would be an experience for you to come, and besides I wanted to try that wall again," said Carlos.

"Glad you brought us," Jim assured him.

"Satisfied about the opening?" asked Bob.

"Sure. I must have been scared. I suppose I passed one of the ordinary openings, and imagined I felt the stone move behind me. Want to—" he paused abruptly as a sharp hissing sound reached his ears, and an instant later a long rope was coiled about him, dragging him to the ground.

The Flying Buddies recognized the sound and jumped aside in time to get beyond the reach of the lariat, and whirled about. The rope was fastened around a low stone, and two men, one large and burly, while the other was smaller, leaped at them with vicious snarls. They dodged aside as fast as their feet could take them, but after a moment the bigger man had Bob clutched about the waist while in another second Jim and the other fellow were struggling fiercely. Carlos rolled and struggled with his bonds, but he was helpless. Caldwell's assailant made short work of the young fellow. One sharp jab on his jaw and he was stretched out unconscious, then the big chap sprang to the assistance of Jim's opponent. He dodged in swiftly, his great fist coming down like a sledge hammer, but Austin was able to duck so the blow grazed his shoulder. With all the strength and speed he could muster, Jim leaped back. He was conscious that the edge of the great cliff was within a few inches of his feet and that a misstep would send him into the abyss below. Crouching he kept his eyes on the two who leered wickedly as they came on, inch by inch, but as they drew close, Jim sprang forward and lighted on his feet a yard beyond them. Then he dared to glance over his shoulder quickly, and backed toward the great wall of the ancient temple.

By that time Carlos was yelling at the top of his lungs, and Austin wondered vaguely why he did it. The sound of his voice echoed and re-echoed eerily through the ancient temple and seemed to die off in a moan among the cliffs of the Andes. Vainly the boy looked for a weapon, a rock or a club, but the winds of the ages had swept the spot clean, and he had only his bare hands with which to defend himself. The two had whirled and were coming upon him again, then suddenly the small man paused.

"Come on, give the bunch of them the works. They got it coming to them, the blasted butt-ins," he snarled. "Shut that howling trap," he indicated to Carlos whose throat must have ached with his efforts.

"All right, Boss. I was in favor of doing that right along," the big fellow sneered and quite calmly the pair drew guns from their pockets. As the small man got his ready, something dropped from his holster. It looked like a piece of torn paper, but the chap did not know that he had dropped it. Austin had his back to the longest section of the wall; the other two boys were a short distance away.

"This guy won't know what hit him," the big fellow growled maliciously.

"Shut the other one up first," came the order.

"Say, what have we done to you fellows?" Jim demanded.

"If you don't know, we ain't taking time to enlighten you, see," the big fellow snarled. Their guns were raised deliberately, and although Jim thought of running, he was sure it would not help matters. He faced the two men and his fists clenched.

"You are a pair of cowards," he taunted them. "Go on and shoot."

"Blast you, I will." The gun was pressed close to his chest and the boy saw the man's fingers grip over the trigger. He held his breath for the explosion, but none came. There was an odd little click repeated four times, then the fellow stared at the weapon. In a second it flashed on Jim's mind that the gun must be empty. He gave a short laugh, jumped forward so hard that he knocked the fellow on his back, his head struck the rock and he lay still, but as he fell his gun flew from his hand, struck the stone wall, and there was a violent explosion, followed by a shriek from his companion who seemed to have found his own weapon equally useless. He dropped in a heap, blood spurting from his side and arm. The turn of events were so startling that Jim could only stand staring in wonder, then his eyes fell on Bob and Carlos, who had been startled into silence.

"I'll get you loose and you can help me with Buddy," Austin said mechanically. He cut the rope that bound De Castro, and the two turned their attention to Caldwell, who moaned slightly, and moved his arm.

"He's not dead," Jim shouted.

"No. Let me help him." The voice was calm, and a tall man stooped over the prostrated young fellow. Jim watched anxiously and a moment later Bob was being raised to his feet. "Feel better?"

"Sure—I feel all right—I say, Corso, how in the name of perforated parachutes did you get here," the boy bellowed.

"We found a way," the man laughed.

"We wished to explore this so famous Amy-Ran," came a second voice and Jim whirled.

"Yncicea—you here and Corso—Gosh but we are lucky, and gee, it's great to see you close again."

"Yes, Jim Scout, you are lucky. Our apologies for not being more prompt to assist you," the youngster grinned.

"What did you do to their guns?" Jim demanded softly.

"That is something I have not learned yet, Jim Scout, but when you are in the laboratory again, ask my esteemed father. You have been having some troublesome adventures," he added so softly that Carlos could not overhear. "You may introduce us to your companion as friends from Vermont."

"All right." It was done in a moment, and Carlos thought the "tourists" had merely happened along at a timely moment, heard his yells and hastened to their assistance. He thanked them with great politeness, and urged them to pay a visit to his home. It did not occur to him to inquire how they got there and they made no attempt to enlighten him.

"Gee, I wish we were staying on while you are here," Bob said cordially. "But we probably have to start Dad home day after tomorrow."

"We are leaving, tonight," Corso told them. Just then they heard an angry snarl, turned quickly in time to see the small man lower himself over the edge of the cliff and disappear from sight. The other chap had not moved, and now Corso went to him but there was nothing he could do.

"I saw that fellow drop this," Jim picked up the piece of paper. It was the same sort that he had found in the old room dug from the root cellar at the Gordon's ranch, and he whistled as he examined the piece. There were a number of dim lines, like some old-time diagram, and only a part of one word—"an" was left. Quietly the boy handed it to Corso. The man looked at it, then smiled.

"This is the part he should not have lost," he announced as he tucked it into his pocket. "Thank you."

"Think he'll get down?" Bob asked.

"He may and we will do nothing to injure him while he is trying," Corso told them.

"We should throw a rock down on him," Carlos declared hotly. "I wonder who the fellow is."

"I believe that he is the last of a gang which was apprehended in Texas a few months ago. At that time he escaped—"

"Well, he'll dash his brains out going down that cliff without a rope," Carlos declared. "I know what it means to get to the bottom."

"Expect we better spread our little wings and fly, my brother," Bob proposed.

"We've lingered here quite a while," Jim agreed. "Hope we meet you again, Yncicea and you too, Corso."

"It will be a pleasure." The Flying Buddies were anxious to get away before Carlos became too inquisitive about their touring friends, so the three hurried along the wild-S and finally reached the "Lark." They piled into the cock-pits, waved to the two who were still standing by the ancient rocks of Amy-Ran, then the motor roared, the plane lifted, circled, leveled out, and started back to the plantation.

"Is it what you would call the completion of a—"

"The end of a perfect day," Bob laughed gayly, then added, "Only it isn't the end, it's only the middle." Soon the outlines of Cuzco began to roll toward them, and selecting the broad drive of the De Castro plantation, the Sky Buddy began to bring the "Lark" down. He gave a happy sigh as she touched the ground, then, his eyes turned toward the north.

"It'll be great to get home," he said to Jim, who had leaped out of the rear cock-pit and was standing under the shelter of the broad wing.

"You bet," Austin nodded.

9 781774 816509